The Autobiography
of
Billy the Kid

as told to
Ralph Estes

Caminos felices,
Ralph
Estes

Black Rose Writing

www.blackrosewriting.com

The final approval for this literary material is granted by the author.

First printing

All work cited and documented based on factual accounts.

ISBN: 978-1-61296-139-2

PUBLISHED BY BLACK ROSE WRITING

www.blackrosewriting.com

Printed in the United States of America

The Autobiography of Billy the Kid is printed in Book Antiqua

Contents

The Autobiography
of
Billy the Kid

My name is William Bonney
And I have some things to tell
All about my life and death
And the way things are in hell
And the lies they told about me
After Garrett shot me down
In New Mexico
In eighteen eighty-one

—Dave Stamey, "The Skies of Lincoln County"

Billy the Kid! Famous outlaw, bloodthirsty killer, scourge of Lincoln County and the terror of the West, a name to frighten recalcitrant kids into behaving.

Killed his first man when he was only twelve, to avenge an insult to his mother.

Went on to kill at least twenty-one men, one for each notch on his gun and each year of his young life – not counting Mexicans and Indians.

Lived in a magnificent cavern in Eastern New Mexico with crystal chandeliers, Persian carpets, elaborate feasts served by one hundred beautiful senoritas.

Chased down and captured, tried, convicted, sentenced to hang. Then shot both his guards in an incredible escape.

Finally killed by his nemesis and former friend, Sheriff Pat Garrett, in a darkened bedroom in Fort Sumner, New Mexico.

Or not?

The story of Billy the Kid has been told many times. Sometimes it's an outlandish fantasy, such as Pat Garrett's own book *The Authentic Life of Billy of Kid*, or the multitude of Hollywood creations – over sixty movies.

Other times it's a work of serious history – except that much of the history has had to be imagined because of conflicting evidence or no evidence at all. So such works often disagree.

This book is not another attempt to tell that history.

This book tells Billy's side. Why he did what he did, what choices he saw, what he felt. His yearnings, his joys, his regrets. Billy's own story, in his own words.

How This Book Came to Be

Billy the Kid didn't die of Pat Garrett's bullet on July 14, 1881. He was shot, but he didn't die.

When Deluvina Maxwell entered Pete Maxwell's bedroom – alone, because Pete and Pat Garrett were afraid to go back in after the shooting – she discovered Billy on the floor, badly wounded. As Billy let out a low groan, Deluvina quickly grasped the possibilities and urgently whispered, "Play dead, Billy, play dead."

Though in great pain, Billy held himself motionless as Deluvina and friends moved and then dressed his body, attended him through the night, laid him in a coffin with contrived air holes, and at daybreak lowered him into the grave. Delays, to reposition the "corpse," to re-hammer the top more tightly, to bring the coffin back up for Deluvina to place a Bible with Billy, led a very nervous Garrett to take off – "skin out" in the parlance of the day – as the first shovelful of dirt fell. Garrett evidently feared for his life, for he was amidst Billy's loyal friends.

With Garrett gone, Billy was brought out of the grave and spirited away to a nearby ranch for recuperation. He eventually made his way to Wichita where he had lived happily with his mother and brother as a child. There, under the name of Henry Carter, he lived to a ripe old age.

Then in 1951, the Wichita newspaper published an article about Ralph Estes, a local high school student. The piece caught one very important eye – that of Henry Carter.

Carter, still living in Wichita but now dying with cancer and in a senior care facility, saw the article and was much impressed by Ralph's analysis. The young lad had captured almost exactly what Henry – in his days as Billy the Kid – was thinking in 1878 at the start of the Lincoln County War.

Henry asked the facility to get Ralph to come and see him. They talked at length about regulator movements and the role of such citizen movements in the quest for justice in the formative years of the country.

The Wichita Eagle
July 14, 1951

Local Student Wins Statewide Essay Contest

Local student Ralph Estes won the statewide history essay contest last Saturday with his work on Regulator Movements of the 19th century. Estes related the 1878 Lincoln County Regulators, who fought corruption by state and local officials in New Mexico, to earlier Regulator movements. Famous outlaw Billy the Kid was a member of the Lincoln County Regulators.

Henry at last decided to reveal his real history to Ralph, but first swearing Ralph to tell no one until after his death.

Over some two weeks Ralph visited Henry almost every day, with a borrowed tape recorder.

As Henry grew weaker he became desperate to finish the story, and the sessions lengthened. Finally he got to Fort Sumner in July 1881, telling of his escape and how he worked his way back to Wichita. Pleading great fatigue, he refused to talk in more detail about his life "after Billy," though those who knew him would later say he was just an ordinary citizen, living and working and becoming a member of the community.

Two days later Henry Carter died.

The tapes were stashed in a box in Ralph's parent's house for years – as a teenage boy other things were more interesting than musty history. But much later, while dealing with the house and residue of his parents' estate, Ralph uncovered the box of tapes. He now realized that nothing could be more interesting than transcribing Billy's true life story.

Except for minor editorial adjustments, what follows are Billy the Kid's own words.

My Life, by Billy the Kid – as told to Ralph Estes

So much has been written about me, my life, the things I did. Of course after 1881 nobody ever asked me because they couldn't. Everyone thought I was dead. And I wanted them to keep on believing that.

Most of what you may have heard about me came from a book, *The Authentic Life of Billy, the Kid*, by the man that shot me, Pat Garrett. Garrett, and his friend Ash Upson who actually wrote most of it, tried to make me into the biggest, baddest, boldest outlaw that ever lived, probably to justify Garrett's ambushing me in the dark.

That book has me, as a 12-year-old kid, killing a man for insulting my mother and a few weeks later killing three Apaches. After that I was supposed to have killed a gambler in Sonora and a monte dealer in Chihuahua City, saved a family by killing eight Indians, killed two more Apaches plus Morris Bernstein and Joe Grant. Pretty wild, huh? Reads like a comic book.

Even when I was alive fantastical stories were written, describing a cave we used for a hideout as a veritable castle where "the young brigand" is "clothed in gorgeous splendor," "surrounded with oriental luxury," and "blest with the loves of female beauties whose charm would shame the fairest tenant of an eastern seraglio." Man!

And on and on: articles, books, songs, movies – over 60 movies! And mostly constructed out of thin air. Wish I could say I deserved that attention, but the fact is I didn't do all that much.

So here's the true story, what really happened at least as it all looked to me, how I saw things, why I did what I did, how I felt. I'll try to not just excuse everything I did, but all in all I believe I pretty well acted with honor and integrity, before 1881 and after.

THE AUTHENTIC LIFE

—OF—

BILLY THE KID,

THE NOTED DESPERADO
OF THE SOUTHWEST,

WHOSE DEEDS OF DARING AND BLOOD HAVE
MADE HIS NAME A TERROR IN

NEW MEXICO,
ARIZONA & NORTHERN MEXICO.

—BY—

PAT F. GARRETT,

SHERIFF OF LINCOLN COUNTY, N. MEX.

BY WHOM

HE WAS FINALLY HUNTED DOWN &
CAPTURED BY KILLING HIM.

☞ A FAITHFUL, INTERESTING NARRATIVE ☜

SANTA FE, NEW MEXICO:
NEW MEXICO PRINTING & PUBLISHING CO.
—1882—

When Billy the Kid was *Really* a Kid

I was born in the year of – well, of course I don't really know since I wasn't thinking too clearly at the time. Haw.

Brother Josie was younger than me, though neither one of us knew exactly when our birthday was. You see, Momma said Poppa had been in the Army and got killed shortly after I was born. It seemed to hurt her to talk about him, so Josie and I tried not to bring it up. I just loved Momma so much, and I never wanted to do anything to hurt her.

Especially at first I think we were real poor, so Momma just celebrated both our birthdays at Christmas. That way she only had to get us each one present a year, and I guess that even then it was probably more than she could afford.

Later on I told people a lot of different ages, mostly because I wanted them to think I was old enough to be taken seriously. Garrett and Upson wrote that I was born in 1859 – and they gave me the same birthday as Upson, November 23. I think I was actually born a little later than that, maybe 1861 or '62, but what does it matter?

Whether I was 21 or 18 or 26 or whatever doesn't seem to me to change anything about my life. Maybe if I had accomplished great deeds of derring-do, they might have been more impressive if done by a younger fellow. But I never accomplished any great deeds.

I know I once told a census taker I was born in Missouri. That's where Jesse James was from, and I thought it sounded like a good place to be born. But I may have actually been born in New York. You know though, sometimes people get a little piece of evidence about where they are from and since they can't know for sure, they choose to believe that. Kinda gives you a feeling of having roots, of belonging to somewhere.

Momma moved to Indiana in 1868 or so. That's where she took up with Bill Antrim. Then we went to Wichita in the Kansas Territory, it was just some cabins and muddy roads then. But Momma homesteaded 40 acres out to the northeast of town, and Bill got the catty-cornered parcel.

Wichita was a pretty good place for us. Momma opened a hand laundry and had good business, she was always a hard worker, and did her level best to provide for Josie and me. Antrim wasn't . . . aw well, I guess the best you could say is that Momma thought there ought to be a man around for Josie and me to learn from, and she picked Bill Antrim even though he was a good deal younger than her. But to tell the truth I never learned much from Bill, except maybe that spending your life out diggin' for gold might not provide your family with a very prosperous livelihood.

Josie and I had our chores to do and Momma made us study some at home, but otherwise we pretty much had the run of the town. What there was of it. Meeting Indians was exciting, and seeing the cowboys come up the Chisholm Trail with their herds. We'd chase each other up and down the boardwalks with our make-believe pistols, and we'd sure gawk at the real cowboys as they come clomping up the steps into a saloon, with big floppy hats and high-heeled boots and real pistols. Like every other kid our age, I guess, I really wanted to be a cowboy.

I heard that those cowboys, or some of them, were prone to get liquored up and rowdy, and maybe start shooting at the gaslights. It must have been pretty rough, because the town quickly went through its first three sheriffs.

Josie and I never saw any of that because Momma pretty well kept us at home after dark, but once we did sneak a peak in Rowdy Joe Rowe's saloon over on the west side in Delano. Didn't get to go in though. And we paid a price: Momma purt-near whaled the tar out of both of us.

She made us remember that the law – *her* law – was that we stayed away from that unincorporated and lawless west side of the Arkansas River, away from Delano. Which of course just made us want to go over there all the more, but after that one whipping we remembered the law.

I heard that Wyatt Earp was a policeman in Wichita a couple of years after we left, and got fired after beating up a candidate for sheriff. That was of course before Dodge City, and before Tombstone and the OK Corral made him famous. I never met Earp, though I heard about him.

I think Momma got on really well in Wichita. The laundry was always busy, and everybody seemed to like and respect her. You know, there were a hundred and twenty-three men, and one woman, that signed Wichita's original incorporation petition. I was always really proud that one woman was my Momma.

I think Wichita could have been a good home for us, but it didn't last. Momma got tuberculosis, back then they called it consumption. Gosh, it was so hard on her. I guess working all day in a steaming laundry, along with the Kansas climate, must have brought it on, and it sure as shootin' made it worse.

So Bill Antrim and Momma moved us farther west. First to Denver, then to the New Mexico Territory. Momma and Bill got married on the way, in 1873 in Santa Fe. I was proud to sign the papers as a witness. Then we settled in Silver City.

One hundred twenty-three men and one woman signed the original Wichita incorporation petition. The woman was Mrs. Catherine McCarty, who owned and operated a laundry. Later, she moved to New Mexico, where her oldest son, Henry, changed his name to William Bonney, better known as "Billy the Kid." (Wichita Metro Chamber of Commerce, *History of Wichita*)

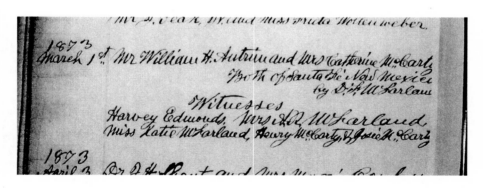

Santa Fe Courthouse record of Catherine McCarty, Billy's mother, and William Antrim's marriage. Billy signed as witness (Henry McCarty).

Silver City

I went to school regular in Silver City. Teacher later told a newspaper that I was a pretty good kid and not a bad student. I think it was true. I got to liking to read, and to learning things. From then on I read pretty much anything I could get my hands on.

Later when I was working as a cowboy on different ranches including Mr. Tunstall's, I found out that a lot of cowboys liked to read, and we were always swapping dog-eared books with each other. Even – believe it or not – things like Shakespeare and Plato.

I also liked to sing, I guess I've liked to sing from the day I was born until this old cancer laid me up in here and kept me fettered. The teacher in Silver City always encouraged me, helped me work up a musical program with some of the other kids for our parents. Then we got to put on a show in Morrill's Opera House. I really enjoyed that. If life had turned out different I might have gone on the stage. Haw.

Did you see that story in Garrett's book, about how I was supposed to have slugged a bully for insulting Momma, and then later stabbed him to death? Shoot, at that age I was so little and skinny I couldn't even hold my own with the other kids in school.

Not that we fought much in school. I got along pretty well with everybody then, always have it seems. I just like to meet people and get to know them, and I think you feel better if you just decide to be cheerful most of the time. I don't mean to be bragging, but you know, even now I'd rather be with somebody who's laughing and cheerful than to be around some old sourpuss. There's this woman down the hall – oh well, I guess you don't want to hear that kind of stuff now.

Momma took in boarders, and like in Wichita opened a hand-laundry. Folks in Silver City liked Momma and appreciated her work, and she made us a pretty good living. Momma had a good head for business.

But even though Momma tried to work hard she wasn't doing well with her sickness. The consumption had a fierce hold on her, and she had to take to her bed an awful lot. Antrim helped a little, but mostly he was off digging in the mines hoping to find his fortune.

Momma hurting and being sick just about killed me. She kept getting worse and worse, coughing up blood all the time. This would make her too weak to work, and finally she just had to stay in bed.

I tried all I could to help, I could wait on her and try to cheer her up, tell her stories and sing songs and put a cold rag on her forehead. But I couldn't do anything about that old consumption, and neither could anybody else. Sometimes when I was sitting beside her bed I couldn't keep from crying. But that would make her feel even worse, worrying about me, so I tried to hide it.

But then on the sixteenth of September, in 1874, Momma died. It was on a Wednesday, I guess I was twelve or thirteen. It was the worst day of my life, worse than my trial, worse than being shot, worse than now that I'm dying.

Josie and I were put out with different families, and I didn't see much of Josie after that – or Bill Antrim either, for that matter. My Momma was gone, and I just felt like I was all alone in the world.

At first I stayed with the Truesdell's and helped in their hotel and restaurant. Then I moved to a Mrs. Brown's boarding house and helped out there. Of course I didn't have any money, or any family there, so I always tried to work and help out to pay my way some. I got to be pretty good at washing dishes, building fires in the cookstoves, emptying chamber pots.

Like a lot of kids that age, I got into a little stealing - first a rancher's butter that got me introduced to the sheriff, and then a dumb theft that probably changed my whole life.

While staying at Mrs. Brown's I got friendly with a feller that everybody called Sombrero Jack. Jack being older I kind of looked up to him, followed him around. My mistake. Jack stole some clothes from a Chinese laundry, and he talked me into hiding them. But, Mrs. Brown found the clothes in my room and the sheriff hauled me off to jail.

I tell you the truth, this scared the tar out of me. I didn't think I had done much wrong, after all the paper said that "Jack done the actual stealing while Henry done the hiding." Kids did a lot more mischief than this all the time, and never got worse than a talking to or a spanking.

But the sheriff said I was what you call an aider and abetter, and he plopped me in jail. I guess I never did like being penned up, and all I could think about was getting out of there. I didn't have any momma or daddy to go to for advice, and I figured the best course for me was just to skin out. So on the second night after everybody had left the jail, I shinnied up the chimney and split for the tall timber.

Course what I didn't know then was that I wasn't really on a path to the tall timber; I was actually heading for the Owlhoot Trail.

Henry McCarty, who was arrested on Thursday and committed to jail to await the action of the grand jury, upon the charge of stealing clothes from Charlie Sun and Sam Chung, celestials sans cue, sans joss sticks, escaped from prison yesterday through the chimney. It is believed that Henry was simply the tool of "Sombrero Jack" who done the actual stealing whilst Henry done the hiding. Jack has skipped out.
Grant County Herald (Silver City, NM), Sept. 26, 1875.

Arizona: My First Killing

I hit Arizona in pretty rough shape. No money, no horse, no experience working for wages, no friends, no prospects. No more'n fourteen years old and all alone, and on the run to boot.

The Sierra Bonita Ranch gave me some work but then let me go right away, because they said I was a lightweight, not fit for the hard work there. It's true that I was sort of little, and of course pretty young, but I tried to work hard and I think if they'd given me more of a chance I coulda made a good hand.

I got some work at a hay camp and then as a teamster, also swabbed dishes at the Hotel de Luna.

'Bout the first thing I did when I got some money was buy me a pistol. Not because I figured I was in any particular danger, but I tell you, in Arizona in those days *everybody* carried a gun. Well, here I was trying to pass as a man, or at least do a man's work, and if I wasn't wearing a gun too then I might just be treated as a kid. In fact, I was often called "the kid" which didn't make me a bit happy, but what're you gonna do?

Also did a little cowboying, worked in a cheese-making place, anything to earn a living. And I guess trying to make a living is what led me into a little horse stealing, I got to running with a rustler name of John Mackie, and that was another one of my mistakes. Stole some horses, got caught, escaped, stole again and got caught again and escaped again.

I guess I shouldn't brag about it, but there was one caper that was a lot of fun. Mackie and I would hang around this saloon called the Hog Ranch and lift the saddles and blankets off the soldiers' horses, and sometimes take the horses too, while the fellas were inside getting soused. Now one day this lieutenant and his doctor buddy were in the saloon talking big about how they had fixed it so nobody was gonna steal their horses or gear; they had long ropes running from the horses into the saloon, and they were holding onto the rope ends. So old

Mackie just gets the two of them all puffed up about how smart they are, buys them a couple of drinks, and I slips outside, cut the ropes, and gentled both horses on out of there. Guess those fellas had to ride their ropes back to the fort. Haw.

Of course a little low-level rustling wasn't unusual in that country in those days. Pretty near everybody did it at one time or another. But I would have been better off, I think, if there'd been somebody around to jerk me up short, keep me more on the straight and narrow - like my Momma would have done if she had lived.

Later on, with Mr. Tunstall, Mr. Brewer, and Mr. McSween in Lincoln I kind of had that guidance, had decent people I could look up to. But early on I was looking up to the likes of Sombrero Jack and John Mackie, not your best role models.

I guess I need to plain out admit that I missed Momma terribly in those days. She had given Josie and me a lot of strength, not to mention some needed discipline, when she was alive.

But now Momma's gone, Josie's off somewhere, even Bill Antrim, as usual, was nowhere around. I didn't have a grandpa, a grandma, an uncle or an aunt, no cousins, no kin at all. When I would make a stab at staying straight, not rustling or anything, it just got so hard to stay with it.

In between lifting horses and getting caught and escaping and getting caught again I was hanging around the saloons trying to build up a stake dealing monte, which I got to be pretty good at. You see, monte's a pretty simple game especially when you're dealing, and the dealer has by far the best odds. So a saloon, I guess always wanting something to draw in customers, would allow me to run their monte table and keep part of the dealer's winnings – had to give the "house" a big cut though.

Then in August of 1877 I had the misfortune of making the acquaintance of Windy Cahill.

What is it about bullies? They act tough but they never seem to go after anybody their own size. By this time I was maybe fifteen or sixteen – like I said, I never really knew my exact age – something like 5 feet 6 and weighing maybe 130. Because of my size and age, I was the most obvious "runt" hanging around the Atkins' saloon in Bonita. There was a big old Irish blacksmith name of Cahill –

everybody called him "Windy" cause he was, you know, so full of it. Always mouthing and bragging. And knocking me around.

I didn't like it and I didn't like taking it, but there wasn't much else I could do. I'd give it back to him in words, then he'd just smack me. Couple of times I tried to fight back, but he was so big and hefty he'd just hold me off at arms length and laugh. Boy, how I hated that laugh.

It would embarrass me, make me mad, but it also worried me that I wasn't acting like a man, standing up for my rights. Though I was trying, I didn't seem to be doing a very good job of it.

Well, one day it came to a head. Cahill was shoving me around, slapping me, calling me things like "runt" and "squirt" and "pissant," "piglet" and "shoat," "baby Billy." I'm getting pretty burned up, but anything I'd say would just make him laugh.

Then he called me a "pimp," probably because my sort-of partner, old Mackie, was running some girls at the Hog Ranch. So I called him an SOB. That stopped his laughing, but it did rile him. He threw me down on the floor and got to sitting on me, hitting me with both hands. It was really hurting, but I was also getting madder and madder, not to mention pretty much ashamed this being in front of all the fellas at the saloon.

I'm down on the saloon floor with my face grinding into the sawdust and the spit and the spilled beer, and I could feel that pistol I mentioned earlier pressing into my side. I was able to work it out, then pushed it into the belly of that big old mountain of hogfat, and pulled the trigger.

Windy Cahill died the next day. Everybody who saw said it was self-defense, sheriff said "I don't care, not for me to decide, I gotta hold him for the grand jury."

How did I feel about that killing? Well, to tell you the truth, I didn't really feel that much about it. Sure, I wished it hadn't happened, but I felt like I was justified and so did just about everybody who saw it. I couldn't shed any tears for Windy Cahill. Nobody liked him, and he wasn't going to be president or find a cure for cancer or anything.

Monte, or "monte bank" as it was often called, was one of the most popular card games of the early 19th Century, particularly in the Southwest. It is easy to learn and fast-paced. The two-card version is called "Mexican Monte," the four-card version "Spanish Monte." Neither should be confused with "Three Card Monte," the shell game played by swindlers on street corners.

There are several versions of the game. One common form is played like this: after shuffling the dealer (or "bank") draws one card from the deck and places it face up on the table. This is the "bottom layout." Then a "top layout" is also drawn. Players, called punters, place their bets on either top or bottom layout. Dealer then turns the pack up. If the suit of the bottom card matches that of the top layout, bets on that layout are paid off. If the rank of the bottom card matches the bottom layout, bets on the bottom layout are paid.

Obviously no skill is involved, by either player or dealer. But players apparently think they can predict the future. As with blackjack, odds strongly favor the dealer.

And things were different then. Men, and especially young men, boys not much older than me, always felt like they had to defend their honor, stand up and "be a man." Otherwise people like Cahill would run all over you. You didn't sue somebody for assault and battery, you fought it out. And if there was a big mismatch in size and strength, then a gun was the great equalizer. Fights not uncommonly ended in a shooting – and it was always considered self-defense and justified.

Anyway, the sheriff locked me up to wait for the grand jury. I didn't cotton to being held in that little oven they called a jail while I waited however many months for a grand jury. So I lit out.

The fellows I'd worked for at the cheese-making place had gone over to New Mexico to farm. Also, there was something in the local newspaper about John Chisum looking for cowboys for his New Mexico ranch. With these possible contacts I headed back to New Mexico. You can have Arizona.

New Mexico: A New Start

I was broke of course, and needed to get some kind of stake. Ran into Jesse Evans and "the Boys," as they were called. Could just as well have been called "the killers."

Didn't actually join up with them, but rode along awhile. Unfortunately, when we stole some horses from a coal camp near Silver City I was recognized and not very happy to see my name in the Mesilla paper.

Though I had now killed a man, and I made sure everybody in Evans' gang knew it, I didn't fit in with those fellas. They were just plain bad. Pretty near every one had a well-deserved price on his head. And they were dealing, and sometimes partnering, with John Kinney – now there was an outlaw that truly deserved the kind of reputation I later got, and never earned. Kinney was mean through and through. I pulled out of there pretty quick-like and headed over toward the Pecos.

On the way ran into some Apaches in the Guadalupes, had to lie low. Lost my horse but kept my scalp. Had to hoof it three days, finally came on the Heiskell Jones ranch.

Up to this time I had been Henry McCarty, then Bill Antrim's kid or "Kid Antrim," sometimes just "the kid" – although a lot of young fellas in that part of the country were also called "kid." When I got back to New Mexico Territory I decided to kinder change my identity. I wasn't real proud of the stains I had put on the name McCarty, and especially back in New Mexico I didn't want to sully Momma's reputation.

Anyway I took the handle William Bonney. Not sure why I chose Bonney, it sort of felt familiar though. Maybe Momma had mentioned somebody in our family name of Bonney – I don't really remember and I'm sure she didn't go into any details that I heard.

Anyway, people still called me "kid" about as often as they called me William or Billy.

Mrs. Jones, "Ma'am Jones" everybody called her, was very kind. To this day I remember her most fondly. She doctored my blistered feet and took me in for a couple of weeks. The Joneses loaned me a horse then and I worked my way up to Charlie Bowdre's place.

Hung around with Charlie, worked for my board, we did a lot of hunting. Frank and George Coe were farming nearby. They were both fiddlers, so we got to go with them to the *bailes* where there were always pretty Mexican girls. I musta fallen in love a hundred times that winter. They were good days.

I didn't know, of course, what all had been happening in Lincoln County before I got there. I did hear bits and pieces but wasn't too interested until John Tunstall offered me a job.

In a nutshell, two men – Lawrence Murphy and James Dolan – ran the county. The Murphy-Dolan store in the town of Lincoln had locked up pretty much all of the beef and supply contracts with the Army forts and Indian agencies. It was a sweet deal, and of course they did not look kindly upon any kind of competition.

The local authorities – District Attorney Rynerson, Sheriff Brady, Judge Bristol – were in their pocket and could be counted on to back them up in keeping would-be competitors out. Not only that, but they had the backing of the "Santa Fe Ring" that controlled the whole New Mexico Territory.

By the time I got there another side had developed: the "cattle king" John Chisum, lawyer Alexander McSween, and English investor John Tunstall. They had just opened a bank along with a general mercantile store in Lincoln, head-on competition with the Murphy-Dolan store.

Also, there was some kind of trumped-up legal case involving the Murphy side and McSween. McSween had done some lawyering for Murphy and Dolan and was now being attacked by them, charged with fraud, embezzlement, what have you. I think it wasn't a whole lot different from politics today.

Mr. Tunstall really set a fire by publishing a letter in the newspaper accusing Brady, Dolan, and Riley of stealing tax collections. Dolan drank a lot and was quick to anger, had already killed one of his employees and had tried to kill an Army captain. So that letter led to Dolan twice trying to goad Mr. Tunstall into a shootout.

The Santa Fe Ring was a group of powerful attorneys, land speculators, and Republican politicians who attained near total control of the state during the late 19th and early 20th centuries, and thus were able to amass a fortune through political corruption and fraudulent land deals. Prominent members included Governor Samuel Axtell; U.S. Attorney General and later U.S. Senator Thomas Catron; and Catron brother-in-law, future Senator and future Secretary of War Stephen Benton Elkins, who was also president of the Santa Fe National Bank and of the massive Maxwell Land Grant Company. The Ring's interests in Lincoln County were fostered by Lawrence Murphy, Emil Fritz, James Dolan, and Fort Stanton Lt. Col. Nathan Dudley.

By this time tempers were hot all the way around and Mr. Tunstall, just starting up his small ranching operation, figured he needed some ranch hands who could also handle a gun. So he hired Dick Brewer, Fred Waite, John Middleton, Henry Brown, and me.

Now I was about 16 years old, pretty young to be riding protection for any man. But I think I grew up fast in the next few weeks. Looking back now, I was maybe getting to be a little bit full of myself – just a teen-aged boy riding with grown men who had already lived through some dangerous times. Or maybe not, maybe I just had no choice. This was the hand life dealt me.

I remember when the sheriff and Dolan's gang "attached" and occupied Mr. Tunstall's store. Fred Waite and I were in the street when Sam Wortley came along with food for the SOBs inside the store. We stopped him, and that led to a hollering match between us all.

I know I yelled something like "Turn loose now, you sons of bitches! We'll give you a game!" Where did that bravado come from? But that's how teen-aged boys can be, figuring they're never going to die. I guess that's why the army drafts them instead of grown men who have developed a degree of sense.

Mr. Tunstall gave me a talking to after that. He was basically a peaceful man, didn't want violence. This kinda toned me down some, which was probably a good thing.

Even though Mr. Tunstall was only 24 years old, he was sort of like a father or big brother to me. He seemed to take a particular interest in my developing into an honest man, and in turn I felt quite a loyalty to him. I hadn't known any man like that before. I guess I would have done just about anything to please him.

Then came February 18 of 1878, the day that changed my life and that of a lot of other people – the day that Mr. Tunstall was murdered in cold blood.

Tunstall is Murdered,
And the Lincoln County War is On

I mentioned the trumped-up legal case against Mr. McSween. Well, Judge Bristol, Dolan's man, decided that McSween and Mr. Tunstall were partners. So, to get at McSween Bristol

```
See  appendix  for
fuller  account  of
the  Lincoln  County
War.
```

issued a writ of attachment against Mr. Tunstall's property. His store, merchandise, ranch horses, cattle, everything.

Legally McSween and Tunstall weren't partners then. I think they had intended to become partners but hadn't done that yet. So Bristol's attachment was illegal.

Then Sheriff Brady, who had already threatened Mr. Tunstall's life, sent deputies to take possession of Mr. Tunstall's store. Mr. Tunstall had some of us who were in Lincoln round up what horses he had there and drive them to his ranch. Then word came that Brady was sending a posse to the ranch to attach the ranch animals, and that the posse had added a bunch of the Seven Rivers gang.

There were usually twenty or thirty outlaws hanging around the Seven Rivers area, down where seven creeks emptied into the Pecos. Most of that crowd had wandered over from Texas, and Dolan could always call on them.

We called in all the boys we could find, including some of Chisum's ranchhands, and forted up at the ranch. We were expecting the posse to attack at any moment. .

If they had come in shooting we might have settled the whole thing right then and there. But Mr. Tunstall wanted to avoid a fight. So he sent a message to the posse that he would allow the attachment of his cattle, even though he knew that was illegal.

Wanting to get away from the ranch before the posse got there, Mr. Tunstall had Brewer, Middleton, Widenmann and me round up horses that had been exempted from the attachment, and the five of us took off across country, through the hills. We meant to drop the horses off at Brewer's place, and then go on into Lincoln so Mr. Tunstall could deal with the sheriff and his illegal attachment of the cattle.

Late in the afternoon – this is Monday, February 18 – we were on a trail through the hills that would take us to Brewer's and on to Lincoln. Mr. Tunstall, Brewer, and Widenmann were out in front, Middleton and I were a few hundred yards in the back keeping a lookout in case the posse came up behind us.

Now comes the part that I've gone over a thousand times in my mind!

The fellas in front flushed some wild turkeys. There wasn't any cowboy in those days that would pass up a chance to bag a couple of gallinas. That's what I always called them, but I guess the right word is actually gallos. You get older and wiser. Anyway, Brewer and Widenmann took off whooping and hollering, leaving Mr. Tunstall alone with the loose horses.

And that was just when the so-called posse, a dozen or more, came swarming over the hill behind us. Middleton and I goosed our ponies and hollered for the others to take cover. Middleton was closest to Mr. Tunstall, and I could hear him calling Tunstall to follow him. But Mr. Tunstall seemed stunned or something. He was jerking his horse back and forth and yelling something like "What, John? What, John?"

The four of us got some trees between us and the gang, then we heard shots. We hit the dirt, heard more shots. We peered through the bushes, and we could see Mr. Tunstall on the ground. He was obviously shot. His horse was also shot. They were taking Mr. Tunstall's hat and putting it under his horse's head. Then they folded his arms across his chest and put a blanket under his head, kind of like he had laid down to take a nap. The killers rode off whooping and laughing.

We considered going after them but we were badly outnumbered; it would have just been suicidal. So we worked our way through the hills to Lincoln town.

That's what my memory tells me happened. But I don't entirely trust my memory. I've gone over this so many times in my mind I worry that I could have painted too good a picture for me, for William

Bonney. But even the picture I think I remember isn't all that good.

Our job, right then, was to protect Mr. Tunstall. We didn't do it, and he got murdered. We knew that gang was on the loose, we knew or ought to have realized that they might come after us. Of course it was a mistake for Brewer and Widenmann to take off after turkeys, although I suppose they could have figured that two of us were coming up from behind so Tunstall wouldn't be unprotected. Maybe instead of Middleton and me riding so far back, we should all have closed up tighter around Mr. Tunstall.

Or maybe Middleton and I should have ridden up to Mr. Tunstall and then faced the gang, and hollered for Brewer and Widenmann to come back. Maybe with five of us, they could have been reasoned with. Or maybe instead of heading for good cover the four of us should have dropped where we were and cut loose shooting. We would probably have all been killed, but who knows. And anyway, wasn't that our job?

Maybe, maybe. One side of my head wants to say I couldn't have done anything better, but the other side keeps whispering "Guilty! Guilty! Guilty!"

What I do know is this. Mr. Tunstall's murder cut a deep scar into my soul, and from that day on I was pretty near obsessed with getting his killers. Was it anger and revenge, or was it a deep feeling of guilt? I don't know, I'll never know.

Back in Lincoln the Dolan "posse" told Sheriff Brady that Mr. Tunstall had turned his horse toward them and threw down on the gang. Now this was the worst kind of nonsense.

Mr. Tunstall was not a man of the gun - that's why he had us along. I don't know this for sure, but he very well might have turned to face the gang figuring he could reason with them. Maybe they hadn't been by the ranch, didn't know he had left the cattle they were after there, he could have told them that.

Mr. Tunstall was like that. But draw your gun on a gang of killers? Huh, even I wouldn't be crazy enough to do that. At least not ordinarily.

The coroner's jury, appointed by Justice of the Peace Wilson, wasn't fooled. Its verdict was that Mr. Tunstall was murdered by Jesse Evans, Frank Baker, Billy Morton, and James Dolan, among others.

Squire Wilson then issued warrants for arrest of the murderers.

Constable Martinez was afraid to serve the warrants, afraid he might get himself killed. Fred Waite and I said we would go with him, so Martinez deputized us.

That was Tuesday. On Wednesday we headed for Dolan's store to make the arrests. Well, it didn't work out that way.

We were met at the door by Brady and the very men we had warrants for, all with drawn guns. Brady refused to allow the arrest of any of the killers, claimed they were legal possemen – and then arrested the three of us! Didn't say what for. But he made a point of marching us down the street to the jail so everybody could see.

He soon let Martinez go but kept Waite and me in jail long enough to be sure we missed Mr. Tunstall's burial service. Just pure spite, something Brady was expert at. When he did let us go, he kept my Winchester and pistol. That was thievery. Made me plenty mad.

Like I mentioned before, there was this legal thing between McSween and the Dolan crew. I can't remember all the details but it was clear that they were trying to arrest McSween and get him into that hole in the ground they called the jail. And we knew that Dolan had gone down to Mesilla to get the outlaw John Kinney to come up and kill McSween, just as soon as they could get him in jail overnight.

So, McSween gets Squire Wilson to appoint Dick Brewer a special constable, and Brewer then deputizes several of us including me. McSween knew he needed protection, but our ideas were a bit more ambitious – we intended to get Mr. Tunstall's murderers one way or another. And after watching Sheriff Brady in action, we pretty well knew it would have to be "another." Anyway, that's how I became a law enforcement officer!

We called ourselves Regulators. In those days that name meant a group of citizens who would undertake to enforce the law and justice when the so-called authorities were themselves crooked, using the law for their own gain.

You know, Ralph, it was your writing about Regulator movements in your newspaper article that first caused me to want to meet you.

Now maybe we didn't always do the right thing, but we did see ourselves as a response to corrupt officials – I like that term – corrupt officials, who controlled Lincoln County and the territory of New Mexico through the Santa Fe Ring.

So with the "official" law, the sheriff, district attorney, county judge all on the side of the Dolan gang, and McSween's life not worth a plugged nickel if they got him into that jail, he wrote out his will and took to the hills.

Regulator Movements

In early American history backcountry farmers, homesteaders and squatters sometimes formed extralegal organizations to defend themselves against corrupt colonial officials, as well as from what they saw as abuse of power by government and economic forces. These came to be referred to as "regulator" movements, and include the North Carolina War of the Regulation or Regulator Movement (1764-1771), the "Green Mountain Boys" movement, Shays' Rebellion, and the Whiskey Rebellion.

The North Carolina movement was probably viewed by the Lincoln County Regulators as a particularly relevant precedent. There a small clique of wealthy officials became an exclusive inner circle, or "ring" not unlike the Santa Fe Ring, that controlled the political power and legal affairs of the area.

We Catch Two of the Murderers

Dick Brewer was now a deputy constable and our leader. He was a good man, maybe the best in the whole Lincoln County War. We went a-looking, headed toward the rat's nest of outlaws at Seven Rivers. We jumped Morton and Baker down near the mouth of the Rio Penasco and, after a good chase, they surrendered. Which, I gotta tell you, kind of disappointed us. We were hoping they'd run so we'd have an excuse to shoot them.

Then here's what happened. It was March 9th, and we had been on the road three days. Our horses were near give out. We were somewhere along in Agua Negro Canyon when Morton grabbed Bill McCloskey's pistol, shot him, then Morton and Baker made a break. They were firing at us as they ran, but we cut them down pretty quickly. That's what McSween said later in his deposition for a federal investigator, and I'm sticking with it.

Meanwhile, Governor Axtell had come to Lincoln and holed up with Dolan, Murphy, and Brady. Doing their bidding, he dismissed Wilson as Justice of the Peace because he had "only been appointed, not elected." Well shoot, that would mean the appointments of the four other JPs in Lincoln County should have also been nullified, but Axtell didn't bother with them.

Axtell just said that all of Wilson's actions as JP were null and void, and that meant that Brewer's appointment as deputy constable and the deputization of the Regulators as a legal posse were illegal. I'm pretty sure that Axtell himself was the one behaving illegally here, just doing the bidding of the Santa Fe Ring and the Dolan gang.

It didn't matter too much, though. We were the Regulators, we had a job to do, and we were going to do it.

You know, I've been characterized as a greenhorn, just an inexperienced kid, when the Lincoln County War began. I was a kid all right, but not so green. For better or worse, I had ridden with outlaws both in Arizona and in southern New Mexico, I had killed a man in self-defense, and frankly after all my practicing I was a pretty dang good shot.

But I also grew, or aged, a lot with the killing of Mr. Tunstall, the formation of the Regulators, and riding down Morton and Baker. Before all that I had been kinda insecure, defensive about my age and size. But now I was beginning be more self-confident, actually feel like a man.

Cutting Off the Snake's Head

Over the next couple of weeks the Regulators were searching the hills and valleys for the other murderers and, especially at night around a campfire, we were pondering what we should do next. Should we continue to try to chase down and capture the killers. And if we did, what should we do with them.

I was pretty strong on following the Bible, an eye for an eye. It would do no good to take them to the so-called law, not in Lincoln, not in Mesilla, not even in Las Vegas or Santa Fe. The Dolan gang and the Santa Fe Ring had the whole territory wrapped up, and their "law" just wasn't going to do anything to their boys.

Anyway, we talked among ourselves a lot about who was most to blame for all the wrongdoing and injustice we saw in Lincoln County. Dolan, Jesse Evans, Bristol, Brady?

The more we palavered about it, the clearer it became that Brady wasn't just an observer in the killing of Mr. Tunstall and all the outrages in Lincoln County. He was a power and a manipulator and a planner.

Shoot, he was a Masonic brother with Murphy, Dolan, Fritz and Riley. Also with the district attorney, the colonel over at Fort Stanton, and of course Catron, the big leader of the Santa Fe Ring. Even with John Kinney, about the worst thug and outlaw New Mexico ever saw.

All of 'em just thick as thieves. Or more accurately, thick as murderers. And there's big Sheriff Brady pulling strings, giving orders, sending out killers and calling them "posses."

If you weren't on the Dolan side, as far as Brady was concerned it seemed like you were just automatically a candidate for arrest, even killing. But if you *were* on the Dolan side, you were safe.

Back in November Brady had Evans, Baker, and two other horse thieves in jail, but just left the jail unguarded and the doors unlocked until "the Boys" could walk away.

Map of Lincoln Town

Old Lincoln town, showing site of Brady killing, the escape route from the burning McSween house in July 1878, where Billy met Gov. Wallace in Squire Wilson's home, and the courthouse from which Billy shot Olinger and then escaped April 28, 1881.

Then Brady had the gall to accuse Mr. Tunstall of arranging their escape, even though it was Tunstall's horses they had stolen! McSween later testified that Brady, when Mr. Tunstall confronted him, put his hand on his pistol and said "I won't shoot you now, but you haven't long to run."

And instead of turning tax collections in to the state, Brady gave them over to Dolan. Given the kind of man Brady was, Mr. Tunstall probably signed his own death warrant when he wrote a letter to the newspaper that spelled out Brady's shenanigans.

Brady, of course, organized the posse that went after Mr. Tunstall's horses, and then chased him down and murdered him in cold blood. Brady's posse included Dolan as well as well-known outlaws like Evans, Morton, Baker, and Olinger.

To cover his rear, Brady *afterwards* produced a copy of written orders he said he'd given deputy Mathews telling him not to allow known outlaws in the posse. Now when does a sheriff need to tell a deputy not to allow "known outlaws" in a posse? Weren't sheriffs supposed to *arrest* known outlaws.

So us Regulators came to the realization that Brady was in fact the wheelhorse, and surely as guilty as his outlaw band that pulled the triggers. Still and all, Brady had the title of sheriff, and the Regulators were split between some of us who just wanted to shoot him and others who thought we would be shooting ourselves in the foot if we did. Might turn the people against us. The people had been mostly on our side up to that point, supporting us, giving us provisions, loaning horses, nursing our wounded. Even so, I'll admit I just wanted to kill the old SOB.

Then things started happening fast, too fast maybe to make good sense out of.

McSween had been hiding out near the Bottomless Lakes, over east of Roswell. Actually there wasn't much of a Roswell back then, mostly just Ash Upson's little post office. Anyway Brady, along with a detachment of troops, had gone to Chisum's ranch looking for McSween. There the lieutenant commanding the soldiers told Mrs. McSween that he would guarantee her husband's safety, swore no one would harm a hair on his head.

With that, McSween decided to come out of hiding and turn

himself in at Lincoln. So along with John Chisum and some others, the McSweens headed in wagons toward Lincoln, aiming to catch up with the soldiers. But, as so often seemed to happen in my life, fate intervened. Heavy rains came and forced them to lay over near Hondo.

Several of us Regulators had been sent on ahead to Lincoln, to be ready to protect McSween when he got to town. We knew that his life would be in real danger once Brady got him locked up. Either Brady would let Jesse Evans or another one of the Boys into the jail to do the dirty deed, or heck, Brady might just shoot McSween himself. Would probably claim he was trying to escape – us Regulators knew something about *that* story.

Brady got into town, followed shortly by the soldiers. We thought the soldiers' presence might prevent a cold-blooded killing, but Brady immediately sent them on to Fort Stanton. Now we're sure of what Brady was up to. He didn't want the army around to interfere with his plan.

We sat up all night, to be sure we were ready when the McSweens started in. The next morning we were on guard in the Tunstall store.

And then. We see Brady and four deputies come out of the Dolan store and start walking east. They must have had a dozen guns between them, carbines and pistols! They were heading in the direction that the McSweens would be coming from. Six of us eased out of the store and crowded behind the gate to the corral to watch them.

We were pretty charged up: "Where are they heading?" "McSween will be coming right down that road any minute, are they gonna arrest him or shoot him?" "It don't take four men to arrest somebody who's already said he was surrendering." "No, and it don't take no arsenal of guns neither." "They're gonna kill him. That's what they're gonna do. They'll make a lot of noise and claim the McSweens and the fellas with them drew down on the sheriff and they had to shoot." "That's bound to be what they're up to. When it's over we won't have a chance to tell what really happened because it's all a setup." "Yeah, they've probably got a gang from the Dolan store ready to come running out claiming they saw everything and the

McSweens drew down first."

Then all of a sudden, just as Brady got opposite our gate, somebody starting shooting. It wasn't me, I think it may have been Jim French. But later I was the one, the only one, accused and prosecuted.

Brady was killed. George Hindman was killed. The other two with Brady, George Peppin and Billy Mathews, made it to cover.

Like I said earlier, Brady had kept my Winchester when he had me in jail during Mr. Tunstall's funeral. By God, I wanted that back. I ran out to get it, French was right behind me, whoo-ee, bullets flying everywhere. I think it was Mathews pumping away. Well, he clipped both French and me before we could skitter back into the corral.

I've got to hand it to John Middleton that day. As we were skedaddling out of town, John stopped, got off his horse, dropped to one knee with bullets zinging all around him, and fired off several rounds at the shooters. John was a mighty plucky sidekick.

The Dolan gang tried to claim afterwards that Brady was only heading for the courthouse – not the two-story job where they later kept me prisoner, but the earlier one over there just east of the San Juan church. They said he was going to post a notice that the district court would be postponed a week.

Oh sure. He needs four deputies and a dozen guns to tack up a notice in the courthouse!

But we didn't get to write the history. Most writers, starting with Ash Upson and Pat Garrett, said we were trying to assassinate Brady, and in a cowardly ambush at that. Well, assassination would, in my opinion, have been completely justified given Brady's guilt in the Tunstall murder and all the other wrongs committed by the Dolan gang. But we didn't actually *plan* on killing Brady. It was when we saw him with a heavily-armed gang that we realized they aimed to kill McSween as soon as he came into sight.

And cowardly ambush? Brady was killed in broad daylight, he was well-armed, and he was surrounded by four heavily-armed men. When Pat Garrett ambushed me in the dark of night I was alone, unarmed, didn't even have my boots on. But Pat Garrett is called a hero!

The Battle of Blazer's Mill

By killing Brady we figured to "cut off the head of the snake." Without a sheriff like Brady to back up everything Dolan did and to block everything we might do to try to bring Mr. Tunstall's killers to justice, the sides in the war would be more even.

As far as we were concerned, Dick Brewer was still an officially commissioned deputy constable and we were a legally constituted posse. And we were holding warrants for the arrest of Mr. Tunstall's killers.

We got word that some of them might be holed up in the Mescalero reservation, so we headed south. After a night in the mountains we got to Blazer's sawmill, laid over at the Indian agent's place there. His wife ran it sort of like the bed and breakfasts you see everywhere today.

Well, it seemed that fate was smiling on us, for pretty soon here comes a rider over the hill. It was none other than Buckshot Roberts – I think his real name was Bill Williams – and we had a warrant for him.

I guess I got kind of agitated seeing that killer riding up all casual like. I was afraid if we tried to arrest him he'd split for the hills and get away, and we might as well just go ahead and shoot him while we had the chance. I'm telling you, if we had done what I wanted we would have been a lot better off.

But no, Brewer told me to settle down and sent Frank Coe out to palaver. Coe tried to get Roberts to surrender, but it was no go. Said if he did that Bonney would kill him first thing. And he was probably right. I despised that SOB and all the other killers in their gang.

Now I hope this doesn't paint me as just a bloodthirsty killer. In those days after Mr. Tunstall's murder I stayed mad, madder than I've ever been since. It just seemed to me that there was no hope of ever getting anything like justice from the people that ran Lincoln County and their cohorts in the Santa Fe Ring. If we arrested the killers the so-called law would just let 'em go. In my mind the only way we

4

could be loyal to Mr. Tunstall, to fairly avenge his cold-blooded murder, was to find and kill the killers and the men that backed them up.

It might be easy for folks now to judge that attitude as wrong, but they weren't there then, they didn't live through the things I did, they didn't see the futility of even hoping for something like justice. Of course I settled down some later, but I can't say today in looking back that I should have had a different attitude.

Anyway, after a while Charlie Bowdre and several other fellas got tired of waiting and went out to arrest Roberts. Bowdre yelled at Roberts to throw up his hands, Roberts answered something like "Not much, Mary Jane," and lets fly with a hip-shot from his Winchester. Now pay attention, this story gets interesting.

Bowdre promptly puts a bullet clean through Roberts, gut shot him, you could see the blood fly from both holes. But does Buckshot go down? Nosiree. He jumps backwards into a doorway pumping that rifle all the while. Man, he could handle a Winchester. One bullet hits Bowdre in the belt buckle knocking the wind and the fight out of him, then continues on its journey until it found, and wrecked, George Coe's pistol hand. A bullet got Middleton in the chest, another wounded Doc Scurlock, one grazed my arm.

Then when Brewer peered over the top of some logs, Roberts got him with a deadeye shot through the head – from 100 yards off! Roberts died the next day, Middleton some years later from his chest wound.

Garrett in his book claimed that I killed Roberts, and I was actually indicted later for that killing. But I wasn't the one that shot him, and in fact I wasn't much in that fight. It was too bad about Brewer, but not about Roberts – he was a cold-blooded murderer and deserved to die.

Even though we got Roberts, he licked our crowd pretty full. Dick Brewer was dead, John Middleton, Doc Scurlock, George Coe, Charlie Bowdre, Jim French, me – all wounded in one way or another, and by just one man.

It was time to back off and lick our wounds. While several of the fellas went back to their homes or ranches to rest up, some of us headed for San Patricio.

Licking Our Wounds

San Patricio was just over the hill, so to speak, from Lincoln, maybe ten miles. Far enough to give us plenty of time if Dolan's gang or the sheriff should head our way, close enough to keep in touch.

I really liked San Patricio. The constable, Jose Chavez y Chavez, was on our side, there was always a monte or poker game afoot, we were welcome in everybody's home, and the senoritas! Such pretty little things, and how they loved to dance.

While we were in San Patricio we learned that Judge Bristol – what a putrid old SOB he was – had called together a grand jury. Despite Bristol's best efforts and outright lies, the grand jury returned indictments against Dolan, Evans, and some others of that gang for the murder of Mr. Tunstall. And they cleared McSween of the charge of embezzlement, with a slam at Bristol for exhibiting "a spirit of persecution."

Unfortunately, indictments were also issued against several of us Regulators, including me, for the killing of Brady and Roberts.

After Dick Brewer got killed Frank McNab took over as leader of the Regulators, but then he got himself shot too. So Doc Scurlock stepped up. Doc had already been commissioned a deputy by Sheriff Copeland, who had been appointed to replace Brady. So that meant the Regulators were still a legitimate posse, an arm of the law.

Didn't help though. Dolan had his posse, and like I've said before he also had the sheriff, district attorney, judge, Fort Stanton colonel, and Santa Fe Ring backing him up. About all we really had was the law of the gun.

Pretty soon the governor fired Copeland in favor of a Dolan man, Dad Peppin, and so Doc Scurlock's deputy commission went out the window. Peppin brought in a gang of Texas and Las Cruces killers, including the murdering John Kinney of course, and commissioned them all as a posse.

To make things even worse, Colonel Dudley had now taken over at Fort Stanton and he sent troops to help out Peppin's posse. Dolan must have had something on Dudley, cause he sure did do Dolan's bidding.

Now that so-called posse wasn't nothing but a bunch of outlaws and killers acting under the cover of a sheriff's badge.

They rode into San Patricio when we weren't there, and because we had received hospitality in that little town they just plain ravaged it. They rampaged through the Dow store stealing everything in sight, then ripped off the roof. They stole money from innocent folks, shot at workers in the fields, busted windows and doors. Even killed a horse because its owner was supposed to be a McSween sympathizer.

Peppin had already claimed that he would turn McSween supporters out of their homes and steal all their property. This is what the law had come to in Lincoln County.

For now there wasn't much we could do, we were badly outnumbered. So with McSween in tow – he would have been killed if he'd stayed in Lincoln – we vamoosed. Through Picacho, down the Hondo, to Chisum's ranch. At the ranch we were attacked by some of the gang, but they couldn't shake us out. Still, we knew they'd be back with reinforcements.

We had a parley, a war council you could call it, and to everybody's surprise McSween wanted to go back into Lincoln and get things settled. You see, while all this fighting and running around had been going on, folks in Lincoln had been complaining to President Hayes to "do something." When somebody told him that the road through Lincoln town was "the most dangerous street in America," the President sent down a special investigator name of Frank Angel.

Angel did a pretty good job, I think. He talked to pretty near everybody, including me. McSween had learned that Angel's report to the President said that most everybody was at fault, but Dolan's gang and the Santa Fe Ring more so. As a result Governor Axtell, U.S. Attorney Catron, Judge Bristol, District Attorney Rynerson, and the Indian agent were all going to be replaced.

So McSween thought it might now be possible to settle things peacefully back in Lincoln. Remember that the grand jury had cleared him of wrongdoing. If Dolan still thought he had a beef against

McSween, they could fight it out in the courts. Of course McSween was a lawyer, and didn't even carry a gun.

Some of the Regulators weren't sure it was a good idea to go back into Lincoln, but McSween was the boss. For myself, I was happy enough. I wanted to get this trouble over with and didn't mind the possibility of a good showdown.

Federal agent Frank Warner Angel's report, "In the Matter of the Cause and Circumstances of the Death of John H. Tunstall, a British Subject," is reproduced in the appendix.

The Five-Days Battle

Tom O'Folliard and me, maybe a dozen more, went with McSween to his home. Regulators were also spread out on the east side of town, at the Ellis, Patrón, Montano, and Tunstall stores. In between us some of Dolan's gang were in the torreón – that was a kind of circular tower that settlers had originally built for defense against rhe Apaches – and the Baca house next door. But long about nightfall Sheriff Peppin came in leading his outlaw posse, John Kinney and the other killers. Still, I'm pretty sure we had them outnumbered and we were better positioned.

That first night and the next day there was some shooting but I don't think anybody got hit. Waste of cartridges.

I later learned that Peppin tried to get a cannon from Fort Stanton but at first Colonel Dudley wouldn't do it – there was a new Congressional *posse comitatus* law that said the army couldn't be used in civil conflicts. So Dudley sent a private named Robinson over to tell Peppin that.

There was some off and on shooting going on, didn't amount to anything, but with Dolan and Peppin complaining to Dudley the good colonel decided that his private had been shot at and that we had therefore attacked the United States Army. Just to show you what a bucket of slop that story was, his soldier had only got to the west end of town, where Peppin was holed up, and nowhere near where the shooting was.

So based on that lie Dudley sent troops with a cannon and a Gatling gun. Our fellas to the east couldn't compete with this firepower, and had to pull out. That's when Dudley turned the cannon on the rest of us in the McSween house. Sent us a message, said if we fired one shot across the road at the Dolan gang Dudley would take it as an attack upon the United States Army and he would blow the house and all of us to bits. Well, *that* sure wasn't good news.

Mrs. McSween went out and tried to reason with Dudley, but he turned his back and refused to talk to her.

Later Frank Coe and some of the other fellas had nice things to say about me during that battle. I can't judge much what others thought, but I could tell when the shooting was going hot and heavy I felt kind of in my element. Maybe it was the adrenalin flowing, but I don't remember feeling scared – not of getting shot and not of dying. You get all caught up in the noise and shooting and everybody running around and maybe you forget to be afraid.

But I could see that some of our other fellas were panicking. Sometimes a man would have his gun pointed at the enemy and he wouldn't do anything, just freeze. Or you'd try to talk about what we could do, how do we get out of this, and one or another fellow would start babbling then crying and sobbing, saying things like "there's no way out" and "we're all gonna die." Times like that I did try to pull everybody together, get 'em to thinking straight. But I didn't really see myself as a leader then, even though later some fellas said I was.

They Burn Us Out, Kill McSween

No kind of leader was going to get us out of this easily. With the army effectively giving them protection, a couple of Dolan's men managed to splash a bucket of coal oil against the kitchen wall, and set it on fire. As they scuttled through the back gate we took some shots at them and made them dive into the outdoor privy. We kept shooting and they kept scrunching down. Whew-ee. You could say they weren't in a bed of roses. Haw.

But our situation was getting worse, and hotter. The fire took hold and, though it spread slowly in that old adobe, soon enough all of us were crammed into one back room that was filling up with smoke.

We did get Mrs. McSween and the other women to take the several children and leave. At least they weren't shot in the process.

I was trying to cheer the fellas up, encourage them, but McSween was in bad shape. He was just coming undone, mumbling that he had lost his mind. I told him we were going to make a break but he just sat there like he was drunk. I remember slapping and shaking him, pulling his hair, trying to get him to pull himself together and make a run for it.

We didn't have any good choices. We could surrender and all get killed on the spot. We could stay and burn up. We could make a run for it. That last one was the least bad, although we knew we wouldn't all make it.

My plan was to wait until it was getting dark. Then me and O'Folliard and two or three more would lead the way, burst through the east gate and draw the fire. Of course we'd all be shooting like crazy, in all directions. I figured that would create a lot of noise and confusion, and the others might be able to sort of sneak out along the side of the back fence.

Well, it partly worked. Harvey Morris got killed with a single shot, but the other four of us made it through, to the Rio Bonito and then into the hills. One of my shots took part of that SOB John

Kinney's mustache off. Really wish I had killed him.

Meanwhile the fellas that stayed behind were making their play. Several got away but four didn't, including McSween who may have been trying to surrender. Don't think it would have done him any good anyway, they were after blood that night and McSween was their main target.

Those fine "lawmen" then got drunk as skunks, made McSween's servants play fiddles for them while they danced in the streets. Broke open the Tunstall store and helped themselves. All this under the cheerful and patriotic eyes of the United States Army, with their cannon and Gatling gun, there to protect the citizens of Lincoln town.

And then a coroner's jury, all Dolan's men of course, pronounced that McSween and the other Regulators that were killed were "resisting arrest"!

After the War

That five-day battle more or less ended the Lincoln County War. The Regulators had taken a pretty bad bruising, and some of the fellas decided to call it quits and go back to ranching or farming or whatever. Most of us, though, were even more determined to get Tunstall's, and now McSween's, killers. And of course to get revenge. Not a very good motivation, I guess, but in those days it would have been plenty for me.

We got the remainder of the Regulators back together and on the hunt. We heard there were some Seven Rivers boys hanging around down by the Mescalero Indian agency, and since we needed horses – we had lost a bunch in the five-day battle – we decided to head down that way to see if we could maybe appropriate a few.

Funny thing happened there. We had met and had been sort of following a posse from Lincoln led by Atanacio Martinez. They were after some stolen stock. Morris Bernstein at the Indian agency evidently thought the Martinez posse were raiders or Apaches, or maybe even somebody with a grudge against him. He went galloping out firing and got shot down. We didn't even see the action until we rode up a couple of minutes later, but for a while I was blamed for that killing too.

That's pretty much the way things were going in those days. I got the blame for a lot of stealing and killing that I didn't do, sometimes didn't even know about. Now I did do some cattle and horse stealing, only way I could survive since I was indicted, blacklisted, wanted, with a reward on my head. But I didn't do a tenth of what they accused me of. Didn't seem to matter what it was, somebody stole some corn, "it was William Bonney, the Kid."

By the way, I don't know that I was ever called "Billy the Kid" until the Las Vegas newspaper started calling me that late in 1880.

The steam seemed to sort of go out of the Regulators after the Bernstein thing. We weren't responsible, but it now seemed like the everyday people were more critical, not supporting us the way they once had.

Doc Scurlock and Charlie Bowdre left, went to work on the Maxwell ranch. Then George and Frank Coe headed up to Colorado. I got to admit their leaving hit me kind of hard. There was no contract holding them, but we had been through a lot and I guess I just assumed we would stay together.

I had been hearing for awhile about how much they needed horses for ranches that had been springing up in the Texas panhandle. And the stores in booming towns like Tascosa needed beef. So some of us made a raid on the Fritz ranch – Fritz had been a partner with Dolan and Murphy – and got us a good passel of animals to take up to Tascosa.

Tascosa was a great place for us then. It was growing fast, rough, full of ranches and cowpokes and sort of a magnet for gamblers and your so-called bad men. Our fellas did their share of drinking, gambling, and competing for the favors of the *nymphs du prairie*. As for me, I was once again doing all right dealing monte.

I was also pretty proud of my ability with a pistol and would surely have been interested in a target-shooting contest with Sam Houston's famous son, lawyer Temple Houston. Some writer, several years later, described a big contest between Houston, Bat Masterson, and me. Claimed Masterson won. Didn't happen though. Houston was never in Tascosa when I was there. But in those days newspapers and magazines liked to print a good story whether it was true or not. Too bad, twould'a been fun I bet. Of course, it would have been nice if that fella, while he was making up stories, had just said I won instead of Masterson. Still, that's pretty fair company.

While we were riding in Lincoln County I do think we were a force for good, even though we did some rustling ourselves. When we went up to Tascosa, the outlaws and bandits just about took over Lincoln. Gunsels like John Selman quickly figured out that the sheriff, old George Peppin, would rather set around in front of his fireplace than chouse down outlaws.

Selman had a gang he liked to call "Selman's Scouts." They were running wild, killing, raping, terrorizing folks, robbing stores and homes and rustling stock wholesale. But things were about to change.

After a lot of complaints from citizens to Washington, President Hayes cleaned house in New Mexico and brought in a Civil War general named Lew Wallace as Territorial Governor.

At first that got my hopes up, but it turned out that Wallace was no better than Axtell. Probably a better writer, though, what with the success of his book *Ben Hur.* But he sure did me dirty.

Trying to settle things down Wallace declared a general amnesty, told fighters in the Lincoln County war to go home, put up their guns, go back to farming or ranching or whatever. Everybody was tired, so it mostly worked.

But his amnesty had an exception. If you were already under indictment it didn't cover you. I had been indicted back in April by the grand jury, so I was stuck. Funny, that grand jury had indicted the bunch that killed Mr. Tunstall, but *those* killers were running free – and I was just plain running.

When I heard about the amnesty I didn't know about that exception. So some of us rode into Lincoln figuring that according to the amnesty all was forgiven. But when Peppin hears we are in town and gets an Army troop to help him arrest us, I could see there was to be no amnesty in Lincoln for me. So I sort of escaped and made myself scarce.

The Tragic Peace Parley

I wasn't very worried about Peppin, even with his Army troops, but Jesse Evans and the rest of Dolan's gang were another matter. Far as they were concerned, we were still at war. To try to calm things down I sent Evans a letter asking whether they wanted the war to continue or were they interested in peace.

The upshot of this was that we did meet, sort of, with an adobe wall between us. That would have been about in February of '79. Things didn't start out well, but then we settled down, finally shook hands, headed for a saloon to work out a pact. We got 'er done, with one of the main parts being that anybody that went back on the agreement was to be shot on sight.

By this time everybody was pretty well liquored up, except me – except for a beer once in awhile I didn't much care for alcohol. Anyway, we were all walking up the road when we ran into Huston Chapman, a lawyer now working for Susan McSween on the lawsuits she was filing against Colonel Dudley for the Army's complicity in the death of her husband.

Apparently somebody in the group had had a run-in with Chapman before this, so words occurred, Chapman stood his ground, and was murdered there on the street in public and in cold blood. Lordy! I sure didn't want something like that to happen, and I sure didn't want to be tarred as a participant.

The bunch headed into another saloon for more lubrication, then Dolan said we needed to go back and plant a pistol on Chapman so we could claim he had drawn, and we had to shoot in self-defense. I quickly volunteered, but soon as I got out of sight I skinned out.

Now Governor Wallace got to work. He got Colonel Dudley transferred out of Fort Stanton. Then Wallace got Dudley's replacement to put the Army to work to try to arrest a whole bunch of people, thirty or forty, including me. But I wasn't ready to be caught.

They did catch Dolan and Evans and some others. The territorial grapevine worked pretty well in those days, and before long I heard that Wallace wanted me to be a witness.

Ordinarily I wouldn't have been interested in being a witness against anybody. You just sign your death warrant when you do that. But I was curious about whether Wallace would apply the amnesty to me if I testified.

I was getting pretty tired of running and hiding. Sure, it's kind of fun when they almost catch you and you get away, maybe fool the posse or the army some. But I had me an idea of a little ranchito that I could stock with a couple hundred head of cattle, grow me a real ranch. Get me an esposa and some ninos, settle down.

I decided to write Mr. Wallace a letter. Said I had been present, saw who killed Chapman. So even though it might get me killed I would be willing to stand up in court and testify as to the killers, if Wallace would see to it that the indictments against me were quashed or something.

I admit I had my hopes up pretty high. Thinking to get Evans and Dolan convicted and locked up for good, get the amnesty extended to me, then maybe I could start a new life and stay in Lincoln County among all my friends.

Still, it was kind of surprising when he sent me a letter right back. Said he could do what I wanted and that we should meet in secret, at old Squire Wilson's house.

> Copies of Billy's letter to Wallace and Wallace's reply to Billy are reproduced in the appendix.

I didn't know what to expect, him being an ex-general and governor and all, but I didn't feel especially intimidated. Remember, I had just gotten through confronting Jesse Evans and James Dolan face to face, two men who wanted to kill me, so I could pretty well stand up to anybody.

I knew it was possible that he could be trying to trap me, so I kept my eyes wide open as I got near to Wilson's old house. Couldn't see anybody else around, nothing unusual, so I went inside and there he was.

Compared to me he was pretty tall – shoot, compared to me most everybody was pretty tall. Thin, kind of skinny. Trying to look severe and authoritative. Well, he didn't need to try with me. He *was* the governor and an ex-general. Had a real ugly mustache and beard that looked like one of those fake stick-on things you might see an actor wear.

I told him I had seen Chapman's killing and that I could testify against the killers in court. I remember very clearly what he said. He said if I would do that, "I will let you go scot-free with a pardon in your pocket." Now I'm sure those were his exact words.

We agreed that I would be arrested so it would look like I was being forced to testify. Might save my life that way. Not certain, but worth chancing.

So a few days later I let myself be caught, and was put in a shed near the Patrón store. Wallace hustled back down to visit me, and we talked again for several hours. It was kind of funny, some local folk gathered outside and sang some corridos, ballads. You know, they were my friends. It was a nice thing for them to do, and it kind of touched me.

Don't know if it touched Wallace, but it impressed him. He later made a big thing out of "the minstrels" serenading me.

Then I went and testified before the grand jury, and they brought back something like two hundred indictments. Mostly against Dolan and Evans and their gang, indictments for killing McSween and burning his home, for killing McNab right after the five-days battle, and for killing Chapman. Also against John Selman and his gang from hell for all their raping, killing, rustling, rampaging.

I shouldn't have been surprised, but I was sure disappointed when that bunch all got themselves a change of venue to Mesilla. Down there they either got "not guilty" verdicts or the charges were dismissed. But my indictment was still alive and my trial was set for July in Mesilla.

I had been expecting the charges against me to be dismissed, but figured Wallace would get to that pretty soon. Meanwhile I also testified in the military hearing on Dudley's behavior, or misbehavior, during the five-day battle. Man, did that turn out to be a whitewash! Just wasted my time.

Back in my shed in Lincoln, I waited on Wallace. But then I got word about what was happening, or actually, wasn't happening, in the trials in Mesilla, and that Dolan had been set free and Evans wasn't even caught. I began to see the handwriting on the wall, as much as I didn't want to admit it to myself. Wallace was flim-flamming me.

I knew I had no show, so I just walked away from my shed "jail" – wasn't locked anyway.

Went up to Las Vegas, which was then the biggest town in New Mexico. Dealt some monte. Picked up money for cartridges.

Didn't need much else – folks were pretty much always willing to put me up for a few nights, lend me a mount, some necessaries. While I usually didn't have money to give them, and they might not have taken it anyway, I did try to do things to kind of pay my way. Despite the kind of big reputation I had gotten, I wasn't afraid of any work – muck stalls, slop hogs, chop wood, wash dishes, anything.

While dealing monte I made the acquaintance of a Mr. Howard. That wasn't really his name, it was just what he was going by. His real name was Jesse James. Said he had heard of me, swelled my chest.

We got to know each other a bit. Went to the hot springs west of Las Vegas, afterwards had us a fine supper at the Adobe Hotel there. That was when Jesse suggested we team up, rob trains, banks, easy pickings.

I was flattered, and maybe a little bit tempted, but the fact was I had never done any of that. I didn't rob stagecoaches or banks, and I didn't kill people for money. But I knew Jesse had, and if I rode with him that's what I would be doing pretty soon. So I gave him the excuse that I was about to be pardoned and would stay in the New Mexico Territory, my home.

Here's a funny story for you. January of 1880, Charlie Bowdre and me with a couple of other fellas went up to Sunnyside, outside Fort Sumner, to pick up our mail. Bowdre got to talking with Minor Rudolph, the postmaster, about all the rustling and killing in the territory.

But then Charlie gets to kind of deviling Rudolph, saying stuff like, "Now ol' Billy here, he can't hardly face breakfast 'til he's killed a couple of men." I didn't mind; that's the way we talked about each other.

But Rudolph is drinking it all in, says, "Yeah, really?" So Charlie ups the ante, tells him, "Sure. Now, yesterday was a slow day for Billy. He only shot one man." Rudolph's ears perk up and his eyes get wide, and he wants to know who, why, the whole story. Charlie's stuck now. He's got to come up with some details.

Quickly pulls a name out of the air, or at least it wasn't one I had ever heard, Joe Grant. "Yeah, Joe Grant was getting liquored up in Hargrove's saloon over in Sumner, and got to doing some big talking. Tried to draw down on Billy, but Billy was quicker'n greased lightning and Grant didn't stand a chance."

That kind of talk embarrassed me. If you're gonna tell a tall tale about me, don't make me out to be some kind of superman. So I cut in and said that actually, Joe pulled on me and fired but his pistol jammed, his gun wouldn't fire but mine would.

Turns out that Rudolph got all excited, started telling everybody that came into the post office about it. Then people began asking me. Well, we had started it, or Charlie had, so we just kept it up. Maybe a week later the *New Mexican*, out of Santa Fe, ran a little item that I had shot and killed Joe Grant, "the origin of the difficulty was not learned." No kidding.

The next month the *Las Vegas Daily Optic* ran a bit longer piece, in which they actually got one part right when they said, "The daring young rascal" – that's me, haw – "seemed to enjoy the telling as well as the killing." There waren't no killing, but Bowdre and me sure enjoyed watching the story go round.

Over the years I've been fascinated by how stories of this fanciful killing became more and more elaborate. Joe Grant had been looking for me. Joe Grant had been hired by John Chisum to kill me – Chisum had offered a $5,000 reward for me dead. You know, that was a lot of money, maybe 10 years' pay for a working cowboy. For that amount I might have just shot myself.

Another version had Grant and me shooting whiskey bottles behind the bar. I got hold of his gun and made sure the hammer would fall on an empty chamber. Later this became three empty chambers. There was a version that had me buying drinks for everybody including an Indian friend, and Joe Grant refusing to drink with Indians, then there were some words and Grant drew to shoot me in the back and with my excellent rearview vision I saw him draw and spun and – get this – put three bullets in his chin bunched so close together you could have covered the hole with a half dollar. Of course some had me shooting him between the eyes.

Here's the best part. If there was a killing there must have been a grave. And it must have been in Fort Sumner. So years later the stories started adding that Joe Grant was buried in an *unmarked grave* near what was supposed to be my own grave. Pretty neat. You can't very well disprove that.

Of course, this was just one of dozens of stories that were later made up about me. As a matter of fact, though, I wasn't doing a whole lot those days. I had entered into a deal with the governor, at great risk to my life, to get free of the burden hanging over my head and go straight. The governor had reneged, and that burned me pretty badly. But I knew there was no use dwelling on it all the time, no matter how much I felt it. Now my main concern was just getting by, surviving.

On the Run

I had been giving some thought to how John Chisum had originally gone in with Tunstall and McSween to set up a bank in Lincoln. Us Regulators always figured we were fighting for all their interests. But after Tunstall and McSween were murdered and things kind of fell apart, we were no longer drawing cowboy wages. So it seemed to me that John Chisum owed us each for several months of work.

I ran into Chisum in Fort Sumner and politely asked him for our pay. I was actually surprised when he disagreed. I guess I was always kind of naive about people's character. Chisum and I didn't exactly get into an argument, but I didn't get any pay either.

I walked around sore at him for some time, then I decided I might as well "take it out in trade," as they say. Chisum cattle were easy to find and easy to round up, and taking them didn't give me any guilty conscience.

Besides Chisum's there were plenty of cattle in the area belonging to, or at least claimed by, men who we had been fighting against in the war. I never had to bother with the cattle of honest folks, folks we hadn't been fighting.

And since the governor wouldn't live up to his side of the bargain, and Dolan's "law officers" had standing orders to arrest or kill me on sight, I had to make my living any way I could. Only choices I could see were rustling stock and dealing monte.

It was pretty easy to attract fellas to my crew, what with the reputation I had gotten from the war and from things I had actually never done, like killing Joe Grant. But I did miss good men like Bowdre and the Coes and Scurlock, and McNab and Brewer and even McSween. The crew I was running with just wasn't the caliber of the Regulators.

Even so, we must have gotten to be pretty good at "harvesting" cattle and horses, since some big Texas Panhandle ranches like the XIT and LX hired themselves a bunch of detectives to stop us.

Long about that time Billy Wilson got involved with some counterfeit hundred-dollar bills and even robbed the mail. Well, Wilson was known to have been riding with us, so of course we, that is to say me, got blamed. I never messed with any counterfeit money, though nobody would have believed me if I had told them that.

Then the Federal Secret Service sent down an agent to find the counterfeiters. Now we've got the sheriffs and constables and their posses, Secret Service agents, and cattlemen's detectives all after us. Oh and by the way, Pat Garrett had just won an election for sheriff of Lincoln County and he joined the hunt.

I guess the people who were promoting Garrett figured that he and I had been friends, and that he would know my ways and where I might hide out. We had never really been friends, although we did know each other, and I guess we had been friendly. I had even done some courting of his wife's sister, so yeah, we knew each other.

I don't know what they figured Pat's credentials were to be sheriff. First of all, his hands weren't all that clean – he had done his share of cattle stealing, rustling beeves and taking them up to Las Vegas to sell to the butchers there. And he had just been a buffalo hunter and a bartender. Also a pig farmer – maybe that was what impressed them. Haw!

There were sure lots of tougher and meaner men around who had proven themselves with a gun. Maybe they just thought Garrett looked the part because he was so tall, something like six foot four or five. So Garrett was added to all the searchers.

Didn't change anything. It really wasn't hard to stay out of their way, simply because they were always in a bunch and a bunch can't travel quietly without attracting attention. Our friends, the folks on the farms and ranches, kept us informed.

One of those doing the hunting, Charlie Siringo, had been provided with a wad of money to finance the cowboy detectives' expedition, but unfortunately he gambled it all away in Las Vegas. His crew was forthwith unfunded and he went back to Texas. Not the brightest star in the firmament.

Even so, ol' Charlie later got kind of famous by writing books, actually making up books mostly, about the real life of a cowboy and then his time as a Pinkerton detective. He even wrote one about me, but mostly just copied it from the Upson and Garrett book.

A posse did catch up with us at the Greathouse trading post. It was sort of a comedy of errors, or maybe a tragedy of errors.

See, that particularly time we hadn't gotten any warning that there was a posse in the neighborhood, so they were able to creep up and surround the trading post. Then they sent in a note demanding that we surrender.

I thought that was kind of funny, so I sent them back a note inviting their leader to come in for a parley. Jim Carlyle was their leader, and he evidently didn't think that was such a hot idea, him going inside with all of us.

But then Jim Greathouse, who owned the house, did a pretty brave thing. He said the posse could hold him as a hostage. If we killed Carlyle, the posse could kill Greathouse.

Greathouse was our friend. We weren't about to do anything that would harm him. So Carlyle came in.

He said they had a warrant for our arrest. I said, "Show me your warrant." He admitted they didn't really have one. So I said, "Then you're not a law posse, you're just a gang. So you can stay inside here until dark and then lead us out, give us some cover."

Pretty soon the posse sent in a note saying if we didn't come out in five minutes Greathouse would be shot. Just about then we heard a shot outside, don't know what for. Carlyle, though, must have figured his men had shot Greathouse like their note promised, and that we would be getting ready to shoot him. So he dived out the window to escape, but the posse evidently thought it was me or one of us, and they riddled him.

Then when they saw what they had done, they all got scared and skinned out. Went back to White Oaks and claimed *I* had murdered Carlyle. And that's the way the stories get started. You don't get a chance to tell your side of the story, it just goes down in the newspapers that William Bonney shot Jim Carlyle.

Still and all, I clung to a thin hope that maybe Governor Wallace would live up to his commitment, and I didn't want him thinking I had killed Carlyle the way the Las Vegas paper was saying it. So, I wrote him another letter.

I explained that I had been in the White Oaks area intending to meet with the lawyer Ira Leonard, who was trying to get me the pardon that the governor had promised. Didn't find Leonard there, figured he must be in Lincoln, so we headed that way. We stopped for the night at Greathouse's place, and woke up in the morning surrounded by a posse. I described to Wallace what had happened, and told him that despite what the papers might say I was not the head of any gang.

Probably just a waste of time. Never heard back from him.

After we escaped from the posse at Greathouse's post, that is, after the posse got scared and ran away, we headed east. In the morning we got to Spencer's ranch and he gave us breakfast. Next day the posse that had run away from Greathouse's in mortal fear, went back there and burned the place down. Then they came on after us and got to Spencer's, got mad when they learned he had given us breakfast, so they tied old man Spencer to a tree and burned *his* ranch buildings down. That was sure some brave bunch of purveyors of justice.

The so-called posse had rounded up all our horses, we were left with just one skinny pony among the three of us. Where to go? Fort Sumner would have been best, but Garrett and his gang would figure on that and with us on foot we'd just be sitting ducks. So we headed in a different direction, up towards Anton Chico.

The next several days were terrible – man, oh man. We walked, slogged, drug our way to Anton Chico, seventy miles in the worst weather you can imagine. Blizzard, snow over a foot deep, cold as a witch's . . . well, you know.

Soaking wet pretty much all the time except when we'd find a hiding place and stop long enough to build a little drying-out fire. If a posse had come on us about all we could have done woulda been to stand there, shiver, and grin.

But, in Anton Chico friends outfitted us with horses. Now we went on down toward Fort Sumner because, not being afoot, we figured we could hold our own with any posse.

By this time Pat Garrett had been to our camp at Portales hoping, I suppose, to find all those pretty maidens, crystal chandeliers, Persian carpets, and such we were supposed to have there. Didn't find anything of note, maybe some campfire ashes is all. The camp was just a low place you couldn't see from any distance, a spring for water, rock corral, and a small sorta cave-like depression in the side of a bank.

You know, they did tell that kind of story about me. Another one was even better: had me wearing a blue dragoon's jacket all loaded down with gold embroidery, buckskin pants with little silver bells, drawers of fine scarlet broadcloth – haw, now how were they supposed to know that? And a Chihuahua hat with a ten-inch brim – in New Mexico wind? – all covered with gold and jewels. If all that was true I wouldn't a had to run – I coulda just *bought* Pat Garrett.

Anyway, we holed up at the Wilcox ranch a few miles to the east of Sumner. Pretty soon a rider comes in with a note from a friend of mine that Garrett was in Sumner. I got this kid, Wilcox's stepson, to ride into town and check the lay of the land.

Garrett spotted the kid riding into town, must have figured what he was up to, grabbed him and made him tell that we were out to the ranch. So the honorable Pat Garrett then makes Jose Valdez, a friend of ours, carry a note to the ranch with the lie that Garrett had already left, was nowhere around.

In Sumner we had good friends and figured with Garrett gone we could spend some time there, rest up, have a little fun. There was plenty of space in the old hospital building. So we saddled up, bade Wilcox "adios," rode into Sumner.

It had got pretty late. We were riding two by two, me in the back keeping a watch out for anybody following us. About when we got within sight of the hospital porch I heard Garrett yell out. Oh hell, where did *he* come from. All of a sudden there was a whole lot of shooting and it didn't take a professor's IQ to figure out that this was not where we wanted to be.

We spun around, headed back the way we had come, east on the Texas Road. When we could see that Garrett and his posse weren't following, we slowed up and then discovered that Tom O'Folliard wasn't with us. Later learned that Garrett and them were able to shoot Tom because he had been riding in front. They took him inside, laid him on a blanket to die, and went back to playing poker. Civilized men wouldn't do that, would they, play poker next to a man that lay dying?

O'Folliard was a good man, a good ally, and a good friend. His killing hit me hard. But I should have been getting used to that, I lost a goodly number of friends and allies in those days. It was just the way things were.

It was getting clear to me that things had changed, and New Mexico was becoming hotter than I liked. We'd just done that awful seventy-mile slog on foot through freezing blizzards, then got down to Sumner and find Garrett's got the jump on us. And lost a good man, Tom O'Folliard.

The Las Vegas papers were stirring the pot with no thought of truth or accuracy. The dang *Las Vegas Gazette* said I was the leader of a gang of fifty men – haw, there were six of us riding together then – and hung the tag of "Billy the Kid" on me.

Up until then I had been Henry, I had been William and Billy, I had been called "Kid Antrim" and "the kid" and even once or twice "Billy, the kid," but this was the first time for "Billy the Kid" that I know of, and it stuck. Journalists and writers looking for a hook seemed to latch onto it.

Billy the Kid, killer of more men at his age than any outlaw in history, leader of a huge gang terrorizing, robbing, killing New Mexicans all over, living the plush life in a cavern mansion. Fooey.

Probably inspired by the noise being made by the Las Vegas papers, Governor Wallace then announced a reward of $500 for my "capture and delivery." Notice he did *not* say "dead or alive."

Caught!

New Mexico had been my home since I came back there in '77. I got along real well with the ordinary folks, and they all seemed to like me. Real hospitable, plenty of *bailes*, always a good meal and a place to stay. But it seemed like, almost overnight, things had changed.

Now people were scared. Garrett, the newspapers, the governor, everybody constantly singing the same song about me being a wild killer, blaming every crime on me, making up stories about killings and crimes and brutality that just weren't so. Little wonder, I guess, that people kind of drew in, getting afraid to be seen with me or to be so hospitable.

Maybe it was the weather, too. I don't remember ever seeing a winter so cold. We were mostly sleeping outdoors since folks were now more reluctant to put us up. Also, we didn't want to put people out too much, cause them to risk getting their homes and barns burned by the real outlaws riding as posses. So we were always cold, always wet, often hungry. Life had changed, and it was not so good.

I was thinking about all of that as we were running. Made it to Brazil's ranch, got some food, rested the horses, picked up a horse for Rudabaugh. His had been shot out from under him. Hung around out of sight, but where we could watch the ranch for when the posse came. Then they didn't come. Couple of days passed, and we figured they might be thinking that we were already in Texas and out of reach. Well, why not give Texas a try for a while, at least until things cool down in New Mexico.

So late in the day we moved out, holed up for the night in an old abandoned rock house near a place they called Stinking Springs. I think that name was because of a bad smell from a creek, maybe oil seepage or decayed stuff or something. Or maybe it was John Brown's body a'mouldering in the grave. Who knows?

Morning come, Charlie Bowdre – he had come back with us – Charlie slipped on my sombrero and went out to feed the horses. They shot him, just in cold blood. No "hands up" or "halt" or "you're under arrest" or anything like they show in the movies. Just three or four shots, Bowdre is bad hit, tries to say something and rolls over and dies. They left him laying where he fell. The body froze, of course, and it laid there all day long.

Now we knew of course that some kind of posse was out there. Didn't have any idea how many. Couldn't see them, the old building just had an open doorway and no windows, and of course the posse kept out of sight, and out of reach of our bullets.

Well, there we were. Holed up in a pretty good little fort, walls too thick for bullets to go through and they're not gonna be able to burn us out like at McSween's house. But it's miserable cold.

We had brought a couple of the horses inside for warmth, and that helped some. But we weren't prepared for a siege because we had figured Garrett had given up on us.

I hollered out asking if that was Pat Garrett. It was. He invited me to come out and be sociable. I hollered back that my business was too confining and I didn't have time to run around.

Figured they had probably got a fire going. I called for Pat to send us in some of their firewood. He told me to come out and get it. I told him to go to blazes, called him, as I did all the time, a "long-legged SOB" – but I was laughing, I didn't really think Pat was an SOB. But he *was* long-legged.

Pretty soon we could smell coffee a-boiling. Boy, it sure smelled good. Almost tempted to go out, hunker down around a fire, have a good hot cup of coffee. What I would have given to be able to do that.

Then up in the day we smelled meat a-frying. I guess they had sent over to Brazil's ranch for some. And there we were, inside, freezing cold, hungry as all getout, no hope left. It was clear that they were a lot better able to stand a long siege than we were.

So I figured it was time to fish or cut bait. We had escaped at McSween's, we might be able to escape from here. If we could get the rest of the horses inside, we could charge out shooting like we had done at McSween's, maybe some of us – shoot, maybe all of us – might make it.

In telling this now, I'm inclined to think that maybe back at that younger age I was inclined to be a tad overly optimistic.

The other horses had been tied outside, to the vigas, so we were able to hook their ropes and start pulling them in. But when we got the first one 'bout half way in they shot it dead, stuck right there in the doorway. That was it. If I had tried to ride over that horse's body the top of the door would have taken my head off.

There were only four of us left now. We had lost two really good men in just a couple of days. I tried to think everything through and I couldn't see any way to escape. My "brave" compadres were doing more moaning and whining than thinking, and it was getting tiresome.

Finally I told them, "Look, Pat Garrett isn't my *mejor amigo*, he'll lie to you, trick you, ambush you. But I don't think he'll shoot you in cold blood while you're surrendering the way some other sheriffs would do. For my part, I think I'll just turn myself in and stand trial. Heck, they're mostly accusing me of killing Bernstein and I wasn't even near him, and plenty of fellas will testify to that."

We argued some. Rudabaugh was moaning a lot because they wanted him in Las Vegas for killing a jailer there, and he was afraid he would be lynched. But about dark he ties a handkerchief around a stick and goes out waving it. Then the rest of us followed.

Got outside, I saw Garrett's pitiful little posse. Told him he'd lied when he said he had a hundred men, and if I had known this was all there was I would never have surrendered.

We went back to the Brazil ranch, spent the night. Boy, was I glad to get warm and get some hot food. And a good night's sleep. Yep, I was a prisoner but things could be worse.

Then we were taken down to Sumner. They buried Bowdre there. Mrs. Bowdre, Manuela, took it real hard, kicked Garrett and cussed him out, busted one of his deputies over the head with a branding iron. Can't blame her for that.

I got a chance to say goodbye, I figured for at least a while, with Paulita Maxwell. Didn't have any privacy, but I was still glad for the chance. I had known quite a few senoritas in the area, some better than others. But I cared a lot for Paulita. Maybe too much, given what happened some weeks later in Sumner.

Paulita was pretty broke up, seeing me there in chains. But I tried to cheer her, told her that this was maybe for the best. I could beat the trial, then I would be free to go straight and come back for her. She liked that. And I meant it. I think.

And I was still just naturally upbeat, always figured it was more fun to laugh than to cry, people would rather see you smile than frown. No sense looking on the dark side all the time.

Garrett loaded the four of us into a wagon, me chained to Rudabaugh, the other two, Billy Wilson and Tom Pickett, tied with ropes. I guess Rudabaugh and I were the guests of honor. Got into old Padre Grzelachowki's store in Puerto de Luna in time for Christmas dinner. Can't say this was the best Christmas dinner I ever ate, but it was a mighty fine one, wild roast turkey and all the trimmings.

I proposed to Garrett that we just cut off the chains and all hang around there for a while. Why bother with going up to Las Vegas, and a trial, and all that fol-de-rol. He didn't go for it, can't understand why, sounded good to me.

Next day we pulled into Las Vegas where we registered into that fine resort inn, also known as the Las Vegas jail, which would be our abode for the night. Quite a surprise, got a new outfit of clothes. A mail carrier said he wanted to see us boys go away in style, and gave all four of us new clothes. Made me feel like strutting. Also made me realize that not *everybody* in New Mexico was down on me.

Newspapers interviewed us. One said I was a "handsome looking fellow, with agreeable and winning ways." Now that was better than that demon image of the worst killer in history, or somesuch, they had painted a few days before?

Garrett got us onto the train for Santa Fe. This was a new thing for me. Trains had come to New Mexico a year or so before, but I had never ridden one.

I said to him, hey Mr. Conductor, how much will my fare be. He laughed, told me that "today you ride as a guest of the territory of New Mexico." That seemed to be just about the level of honor that I deserved.

In shackles or not, I was looking forward to my first train ride. You might be thinking, probably your last one too, but I didn't see it that way.

While we were getting loaded up, though, a crowd started gathering and getting mean-acting. They wanted Dave Rudabaugh, wanted to hang him high. This brouhaha didn't really concern me, but

He did look human, indeed, but there was nothing very mannish about him in appearance, for he looked and acted a mere boy. He is about five feet eight or nine inches tall, slightly built and lithe, weighing about 140; a frank open countenance, looking like a school boy, with the traditional silky fuzz on his upper lip; clear blue eyes, with a rougish snap about them; light hair and complexion. He is, in all, quite a handsome looking fellow, the only imperfection being two prominent front teeth slightly protruding like squirrel's teeth, and he has agreeable and winning ways.

Las Vegas Gazette
Dec. 28, 1880

if there was to be a fight I wanted to be in on it. I told Garrett to give me my Winchester and I'd lick the whole lot.

Pat wasn't taking my advice in those days, but he did tell the crowd if they fired a shot he would unloose every prisoner and arm him. Sounded like a good plan to me, maybe not so good to the crowd because then they calmed down and began to back off.

So, the train rolled out to Santa Fe, the territorial capital. It's a real pretty trip. If you haven't taken it you should. You pull south from the station there in Las Vegas, which is a mighty swell-looking building. Saw a lot of snow everywhere except on the train tracks. I asked about that, conductor said they have a little engine that goes ahead just for clearing snow. Imagine that.

South and west, past the mesas and mountains covered with snow, pine trees, pretty little stream alongside – somebody said that was Tecolote Creek. Past the Pecos Pueblo, through Apache Canyon, over Glorieta Pass. That's where they had the last big battle of the Civil War. Yankees won.

All the time that ol' engine's just a-puffing and throwing smoke, chook-a-choo, chook-a-choo, chook-a-choo. You can lean out the window on a curve and see the engine and the caboose both. Then Garrett would nudge me with his Winchester and make me pull my head back in. What? Did he think I was going to jump?

I made up my mind that when this was all over, I was going to ride that train all the way to wherever it went. A horse is good, but a train is *luxury*.

Santa Fe is a real old town, lots older than Lincoln or Silver City, even Wichita. With the Spanish it goes back to the early 1600s, but Indians were there for hundreds of years before.

For all that, Santa Fe didn't look too impressive. I guess when they came in over the Santa Fe Trail from Missouri after months of slogging, it might have looked pretty good, but in 1881 it was really just a bunch of one-story adobe buildings around a muddy plaza. Even the "palace of the governors" was just a long one-story 'dobe. They did have some impressive-looking churches, though, lots bigger and fancier than anything in Lincoln County.

Their jail wasn't very impressive either, and the jailer was a pirate. Stole the meals sent down for us and ate 'em himself. Hard to find an honest man in New Mexico Territory.

Being so close I thought maybe the governor might come and see me again, hear my story, so I sent him a short letter telling him I'd like to see him. Turned out he was gone for a month. Too bad.

> Copy of original letter from "Santa Fe Jail" to Governor Wallace, March 2, 1881, is in the appendix.

So Rudabaugh, Wilson, and I got busy digging our way out. Didn't have any real tool, of course, but we made do with spoons and such. Stashed the sand and rocks in the bed ticking. Beds were so lumpy it wouldn't have affected our sleep much. And we weren't getting a lot of sleep at night anyway, busy digging.

We had bribed the trustee watching us to keep him quiet, but he told the sheriff and that ended that. Just as crooked as the jailer.

Then they put me in a cell by myself. Couldn't dig, so I wrote the governor again. Hinted that I had some letters from him that I might have to turn over to "interested parties." No answer.

Wrote another letter a little clearer, reminding him that I had done everything I had promised him I would do, and the governor had not done what he had promised. The day before I was to be taken to Mesilla for trial I tried one more time. Same outcome.

I always wondered whether the letters got through, and if they did what Governor Wallace could be thinking. If I had turned over the stuff I had to the newspapers it would have looked bad for him. I've wondered whether he was just too much distracted by the book he was writing, putting all his time into it. No way to know now, but it was sure strange that he never responded.

End of March I was put back on a train, with guards of course, for the trip down the Rio Grande to Las Cruces. Another pretty ride, but different. Passed by several mountain ranges, down south the trees were starting to come out, flowers, river running strong. I think last time I had been in this area I left on a stolen horse, now I'm on an *iron* horse. Haw!

Then a stagecoach over to Mesilla. That's where they had gotten a change of venue to for my trial. Old Judge Bristol wasn't about to have me tried in Lincoln, said they couldn't get a jury that wasn't on my side.

Bob Olinger was one of the guards going down to Mesilla. Bob was just another one of those outlaws that in those days switched sides from illegal to legal, back and forth. Before this I would run into him from time to time always riding with some outlaw gang, mostly the Seven Rivers bunch. He was a bad killer and had been on the Dolan side all along, but I particularly despised him for the way he had gunned down Ma'am Jones' son John after the war.

Of course I had shot his buddy Bob Beckwith in escaping from the McSween house fire, so he didn't like me any better. Trouble was, this time he had the badge and the gun and got to shove me around at will. Coming into Mesilla he told me I could just tell my friends goodbye, because I wouldn't be seeing them much longer.

Ah, but the tide does have a way of turning or, as I told him, "Bob, you know there's many a slip twixt the cup and the lip." I had read that somewhere.

The Trial

My trial would be before Judge Warren Bristol. Too bad, I've told you about him earlier. Bosum buddy of my enemies.

Still, things didn't start out so bad. There was a federal indictment for the killing of Buckshot Roberts. I didn't shoot Roberts. But we never got to that, because there was some wrangling about jurisdiction and finally the indictment was dismissed on the grounds, I think, that the federal government didn't have jurisdiction over the Blazer's Mill area; it wasn't Indian land.

I thought my court-appointed lawyer Ira Leonard, Judge Leonard he was called, did a pretty good job getting that indictment dropped. Then they brought up the Brady killing on a territorial indictment, and were going ahead with that. But all of a sudden the judge dismissed Leonard and two new fellows were assigned to me. There was a man named Bail, whom I didn't know, and Albert Jennings Fountain who was another big buddy of Dolan.

I'm thinking, man, I don't have a friend in sight. This isn't going to be a fair trial, I don't stand a chance with the judge, the prosecutor, and my own, so-called, lawyers on the other side. And as if that wasn't enough, these same men put their heads together and selected the jury, being sure, I have no doubt, that every one of the jury would vote the "right" way.

Of course if there had been any justice in the territory of New Mexico this trial would never have taken place, because Governor Wallace would have granted me a pardon.

And of course there were six Regulators behind that wall when Brady was killed, so how come I was the only one on trial. Said they hadn't caught any of the others, but I'm thinking they didn't try nearly as hard for them as they did for me. I've always asked myself, how come?

Anyway, things now began to happen fast. All the testimony went against me. Except that nobody testified they had seen me shoot at

Brady, and Mathews testified that all he saw me do was run out to try to get back my Winchester. And got myself shot in the process.

Next old Judge Bristol gave his instructions to the jury, said it didn't matter whether I shot at Brady or anybody that day, if I was just there they should find me guilty of murder in the first degree. Which, of course, they did.

Ahh, it was just a farce, a joke, except I wasn't laughing.

I think Judge Bristol had been rehearsing his next little speech from the beginning, sentencing me to hang. Don't know why they didn't just go ahead and do it in Mesilla, save some money, but instead I was to be taken to Lincoln. Maybe they wanted the folks in Lincoln to have a show. Well, I'm glad they did send me there, and I guess the folks got a show all right.

The said William Bonney, alias Kid alias William Antrim be hanged by the neck until the body be dead.

Put me in a wagon guarded by that big ape Bob Olinger, plus about the worst outlaw in the territory, John Kinney, who's now a deputy. And several more.

In Lincoln I was stashed in the new courthouse there, second floor, room on the northeast side. You can go there and see it yourself today. At least this was a lot better than that little old dungeon, that hole in the ground I had been in before.

Garrett put Olinger and James Bell to guarding me, told them to never leave me alone and to watch me like a hawk because I was pretty slippery. I thanked him for the compliment but he just told me to behave or I would be dead before the folks got a chance to see me dangle.

Lincoln courthouse where Billy was held – and escaped. His room/cell was where the window is circled, the same window from which he shot Olinger.

Escape From Lincoln

It didn't take long before Bob Olinger had a chance to eat his words – he shoulda told his own friends goodbye.

Garrett took off to go serve some warrants or something over to White Oaks. Seemed like almost an insult to me, like I wasn't important or dangerous enough for him to have to pay attention to. But whatever his reason, I figured this would be my only chance to escape the noose.

So Pat's gone but I still got Olinger and Bell to deal with. Then – I almost couldn't believe it – Olinger told Bell to watch me like a hawk, got the other prisoners together and took them over to the Wortley Hotel to eat. That just left me and Bell, and I knew I'd never get another setup this good.

We got out the cards and started messing around, trying to play some poker. Pretty soon I told Bell I had to go to the privy. He unlocked my leg shackles from the floor and started toward the stairs, but I told him I had serious business and needed one hand loose. So he unlocked one handcuff. That wasn't especially unusual, but this was the first time it happened with only one guard present.

When I came out of the outhouse Bell has me go in front of him, as usual. Got to the stairs took a couple of steps and then charged up to and around the landing. Caught Bell by surprise so I had a lead on him of several steps, time enough for me to get out of sight around the corner at the top of the stairs. Bell come a-rushing around that corner and I got a good swing with the one dangling handcuff, whomped him hard across the forehead. The chain length gave a lot of momentum and it was a pretty good lick.

Bell was stunned and staggered against the wall, I was able to grab his pistol. Ordered him to stand, but he started stumbling down the stairs hollering. He wouldn't stop, so I had to shoot him. He fell down out in the yard, and died.

I figured Olinger would hear the shots, reckoning Bell had shot me trying to escape. I hoped he was worried that he was being cheated out of the pleasure of shooting me himself, since he had been itching for a chance all the way up from Mesilla. So, since I did have kind of a poetic streak in me, I got Olinger's shotgun out of Garrett's office and poked my head out the window. Yup, there was Bob come a-running. I think I said "Hello, Bob," or something like that, then let him have both barrels.

I felt bad about having to kill Bell. We had been friendly before the arrest, and while he was guarding me he took care to see that the shackles and handcuffs weren't too tight, that I got decent food and so on. We sat and talked a lot, and occasionally played cards. If there had been any other way I wouldn't have killed him.

Now I didn't go looking for Olinger to kill him, but when it became necessary I did it with no remorse. Olinger was another one of those bully boys quick to shove somebody around, quick to kill. You know, after he was dead his mother told a newspaper, "My son Bob was a killer from the cradle to the day he died, and he got just what he deserved." I guess today you would call that "tough love."

Then, of course, I worked on the leg shackles awhile. Could only get one off, so I told old man Gauss, he was sort of a gardener and caretaker around the courthouse and had been the cook on Tunstall's ranch when I was working there, I asked him to get me a horse.

Well, he did, but it was only 'bout half broke. When I tried to climb on with a leg shackle and chain dangling from one foot he just naturally spooked and sent me sprawling. I know this sounds dumb, but I was laying there laughing like a fool. I had this vision of Billy the Kid the great outlaw and all-around dangerous man, flat on his back in the middle of the road with my gun six feet away, can't even get on a horse to escape my hanging.

Fortunately no one came a-running to put the gun on me and get a reward, so I finally got on and trotted out of town. I was able to borrow another horse at the Block ranch, and I sent that little uneducated bronc back to its owner in Lincoln.

The death warrant that wasn't served: "I hereby certify that the within warrant was not served owing to the fact that the within named prisoner escaped before the day set for serving said warrant. – Pat F. Garrett, Sheriff, Lincoln County, New Mexico"

So now I'm free, sort of. There's an indictment hanging over my head, plus two new killings. I had to do those killings, but the law wouldn't care about my reasons. Don't know if there was still a reward out for me since Garrett had already collected that.

No money, not that I ever needed much except for cartridges. No job, couldn't get one because I would have just been a sitting duck, and besides that would put any employer at risk with the law. I could always support myself by expropriating a few head of cattle, but the noose was drawn pretty tight around me even though I had escaped the hanging.

I can't say I was morose or anything, it always seemed to me that every new morning was full of opportunities. Or maybe I was just too young, or dumb, to completely realize what kind of a fix I was in. I was laying up at cow camps and sheep ranches here and there, still able to do a little card dealing, drop in on a dance or two.

Still, I did a lot of thinking, and it seemed like the only path left was to head out, to Texas or old Mexico or Kansas.

Couple of months of this and my mind was pretty well made up to go, somewhere. But a gentleman would not just run off without properly saying goodbye. That's why I decided to sneak back into Fort Sumner, give a proper *adios mi amor* to a senorita or two.

July 14, 1881: Quien Es?

I figured I'd drop down to Fort Sumner, visit some folks the next day and maybe there would be some dancing that night. Thought I'd spend the night at my friend Jesus Silva's place, so I went there first.

We talked awhile, about Pat Garrett, and the Santa Fe Ring, and Jesus's goats. Had some frijoles and tortillas and coffee. Around 11 or so, I told Jesus the frijoles were good but I could really use some meat.

Jesus said he was sorry he didn't have any meat, but Pete Maxwell had butchered a calf that morning and it was hanging to cure on Pete's porch. Gave me an old butcher knife, you know how those old knives would have been sharpened so many times the blade was only about half an inch wide. I headed out across the yard towards Pete's porch.

I just had on my socks, no boots, no hat. And no gun, which I guess was my really big mistake. I know that Garrett later told everybody that I had a gun, but of course he would say that to cover his hide. See, I had just been palavering with Jesus Silva for a couple of hours – had my boots, hat, gunbelt all off. I'm going out in the dark to attack a dead calf. I don't need a gun for that.

I just didn't think about it because I knew, or I thought I knew, that Garrett and his posses were nowhere around.

Funny thing about that gun story. A year or so later Garrett sold a pistol he claimed was mine, for $13! Now with all the hullabaloo that pistol would have brought probably thousands of dollars – *if* it had been mine. Not $13.

Anyway, it was a full moon, and when I came through the gate at Pete's place I caught a glimpse of a couple of fellas in the shadows. Couldn't make out who they were, just standing there by the porch. One of them said something, maybe "buenos noches" or the like, but I didn't recognize the voice.

So I quickly ducked into Pete's room and said – well, I honestly don't remember what I said, but it was later reported that I said 'quien es, quien es,' 'who is it?' I think I heard Pete mumble or whisper something.

And then . . . Well, I know there was a shot, which missed me, then a flash and I felt like my chest had exploded, like it was on fire. I'm falling, chest hurting bad. Laying there on my face, can't move, and next thing I hear Deluvina Maxwell whispering real urgent like, telling me to lay still and play dead.

What I didn't know, but Deluvina did, was that Pat Garrett and Pete Maxwell were both scared to death. They knew I had a lot of friends in Sumner. And neither one would come back in the room, evidently afraid I might not be dead and was waiting for them.

So Deluvina – man, that woman could think fast – she shushes me, then runs out and starts pounding Garrett in the chest yelling "You piss pot, you SOB, you've killed my Billy." I'm not making this up, those were her exact words according to others that heard her.

She gets a couple of friends, Vicente Otero and Jesus Silva, to quickly hammer together a coffin, leaving some good breathing cracks. Then they put me in it, tack the top on, and keep a watch over me until they carry me out and put me down in the grave.

They later told me what all happened next. Garrett and Maxwell were hiding in a closed room. I guess Garrett was too nervous to try to arrange for a photograph, although sheriffs in those days sure did like to get a picture of any outlaw they had killed, get it in the magazines and such.

So they started to toss in dirt, calling to Garrett to come out. He does, but they say he was looking around for trouble more than he was looking in the grave.

One fella decides the top isn't tight, drops into the grave with a hammer, throws out some of the dirt, bangs away with the hammer.

Then they shovel in more dirt. Next Deluvina hollers for the men to stop and open up the coffin so she can put a Bible in. She wasn't going to let her "Billito" meet his maker without a Bible.

The men start shoveling the dirt back out. Garrett cusses and, along with his two men and looking back over his shoulder the whole time, takes off.

They fussed around the grave until dark, sometimes shoveling, sometimes resting, sometimes carving a name board. After dark they brought me out, very gently for I'm still hurting mightily, hide me in Deluvina's room for a few days until I'm healed enough they can move me in a wagon. Buried the empty coffin, put a marker on it, "Here lies Billy the Kid," or whatever.

I laid out a couple of months at a ranch outside of Sumner, then was taken to another ranch up above Las Vegas. After I was pretty well healed they got me on the train at Raton and sent me to Wichita. My second train ride, better even than the first cause now I'm a free man again, even if I do hurt like crazy!

I had good memories of Wichita from before. I had run the streets when Momma had a laundry there, so it was about the first place that come to my mind when thinking about where to go.

Friends in Sumner had pointed me to a ranch out north of Wichita a few miles, and the folks there immediately took me in. I adopted the name Henry Carter, which wasn't very hard for me to remember. Haw.

I couldn't do heavy work for a while, told them I'd gotten gored by a bull. They knew different, though. Still, they let me just help out till I was able to pull my weight.

That made me want to work real hard, and I did. But I had some trouble holding my anger in check. I would fantasize about going back and cleaning out Lincoln. And if anybody crossed me my first thought was "Hey, do you know who I am? I'm Billy the Kid." But I was trying *not* to be Billy the Kid, so I couldn't depend on my reputation and stare people down, or pull a six-gun.

Gradually those kind of thoughts faded away. And after a few years the foreman leaves and the owner gives me the job. I'm so grateful I just work all the harder. Eventually the owner gets old and frail, decides to move into town, so he takes my note and sells out to me at a fair price. With that good start I was able to become a pretty successful rancher, eventually got myself elected to the County Commission.

I still miss Momma so much after all these years, she was just a wonderful lady and mother. I wanted to do something to commemorate her memory. So I was able to endow a small scholarship in her name at Wichita State University, and they put up a plaque in the student center that tells of her important contribution as the only woman on Wichita's incorporation papers. You can go over there today and read that plaque.

I don't imagine Momma would have been too happy with the way things developed after she died, at least up until I was supposedly killed. She raised me and Josie to be decent and always do the right thing.

I tried to walk the straight and narrow, but I gotta tell you that wasn't so easy for an orphan kid in the West in the 1870s. I would try, but sometimes I would get in with the wrong fellas and just follow them. But now the Lincoln County War, that was different. I think Momma would have understood about that.

When Mr. Tunstall was murdered in cold blood, just for trying to compete in business with Murphy and Dolan, I believe Momma, if she had been alive then, would have said, "You boys have got to do something, you've got to fight back." And that's what we were trying to do.

I never dreamed it would build into such a story, a legend. All the books and articles, the songs and movies and TV shows. Making me into the biggest and baddest outlaw in Western history.

The Eastern newspapers and dime novelists and magazines seemed to be fascinated with the West, and prone to build up every event and everybody there with stupendous exaggeration. In fact, a lot of outright lies.

> "They harnessed up my ghost, and made it sing and dance. And I am dancing still, I am dancing still."
> Dave Stamey, *The Skies of Lincoln County*

Most of what came after Garrett shot me didn't look like me at all. So I guess there was me, William Bonney sometimes called Billy the Kid, before I disappeared. And there was a Billy the Kid afterwards, a creation of the legend-makers. Not recognizable as me.

Then there were the pretenders. People who claimed they were me, that I hadn't really been killed in 1881. Of course, they got that part right.

Back in the '30s fella name of John Miller talked that around some. Then here lately a man down in Texas, I think he was called Brushy Bill Roberts, has been telling the same story.

But why on earth would anybody do that. Here I've spent most of my life doing my best to hide who I am – or used to be.

But I didn't really care, didn't cost me anything. Sometimes I would get worried, though, that maybe some old friend from Fort Sumner would get mad and jump up and put the lie to a pretender by telling all about me, how I survived and came to Wichita and all. Man, I didn't want that to happen.

That kind of stuff seems to have quieted down now. And with the condition I'm now in it probably doesn't matter anyhow.

So I've told you my real life. Course it wasn't so eventful after 1881, but that's just the way I wanted it.

Anyway, I thought maybe folks might be interested in my story, my side of things. How I felt. Why I did what I did. I hope it hasn't come out as whining or too much self-justification.

I hope people will see that while I wasn't an angel, I wasn't a total devil either.

I was just a young kid, cast adrift and trying to do what's right.

At least mostly.

List of Appendices

I. Who Was Who

II. Significant Places

III. The Lincoln County War, in short

IV. Frank Warner Angel Report, Department of Justice: In the Matter of the Cause and Circumstances of the Death of John H. Tunstall, a British Subject

V. Frank Warner Angel Report, Department of Justice: In the Matter of the Lincoln County Troubles, To the Honorable Charles Devens, Attorney General

VI. Selected Books

VII. Original letters

Text of following letters:

Letter March 13, 1879, W. H. Bonney to Governor Lew Wallace offering to testify against Chapman murderers if indictments against him are dismissed

Letter March 15, 1879, Lew Wallace to W.H. Bonney ("I have authority to exempt you from prosecution if you will testify to what you say you know")

Letter March 2, 1881 Wm. H. Bonney to Gov. Lew Wallace ("I wish you would come down to the jail and see me – it will be in your interest")

Who Was Who

Angel, Frank Warner
New York lawyer assigned as federal agent by the U.S. Department of Justice, to investigate and report back on the death of William Tunstall and conditions in Lincoln County. Angel interviewed a large number of people and produced two reports (below in this appendix) supported by a file of over 900 pages. He survived this most dangerous mission, and died in the East in 1906.

Antrim, Josie
Billy's older brother; they parted after their mother died when Billy was about 12 or 13. Met briefly with Pat Garrett in 1882; they parted amicably. May have later dealt faro, been a numbers runner, clerked in cigar store and hotel. Died in Denver in 1930, age listed as 76, place of birth not given.

Antrim, William
Became Billy's stepfather when he married Catherine McCarty in Santa Fe, in 1873. Seldom around, after Catherine's death he left Silver City to prospect and mine in Arizona, died in California in 1922. Apparently no contact with Billy after Silver City.

Bell, James
A former Texas Ranger, Bell was a member of several posses that chased Billy the Kid and, as one of Pat Garrett's deputy sheriffs, was assigned with Bob Olinger to guard Billy until his scheduled hanging. Bell was killed, along with Bob Olinger, during Billy's escape at Lincoln on April 28, 1881. Billy had friendly feelings toward Bell, said he regretted having had to shoot him.

Bernstein, Morris

Clerk at Mescalero Indian Agency. He was killed August 5, 1878, apparently by Atanacio Martinez who was heading a posse chasing after stolen stock. Martinez later admitted to the killing, claiming self-defense, and was not prosecuted. Regulators were trailing the Martinez posse and did not appear to be involved in the shooting, but nevertheless four Regulators including Bonney were indicted but never prosecuted.

Boys, the

A gang active in southern and southeastern New Mexico Territory in the late 1870s. Initially referred to a band of rustlers led by Jesse Evans, but as Evans became heavily involved on James Dolan's side of the Lincoln County War the term came to be applied to all the fighters on that side.

Bowdre, Charles

A small-time rancher in Lincoln County who became a member of the Regulators and a close friend to Billy the Kid. Bowdre was killed by Pat Garrett's posse at Stinking Springs on December 23, 1880, possibly being mistaken for Billy as he stepped out to feed the horses.

Brady, William

Former military officer and Lincoln County sheriff, firmly aligned with the Murphy-Dolan side in the Lincoln County War. Brady had appointed the posse, some members of which pursued and murdered John Tunstall. He was killed on the street of Lincoln by a group of six Regulators firing from ambush on April 1, 1878, at the age of 48. Billy the Kid was ultimately convicted of murder in Brady's killing, and sentenced to hang; none of the other present Regulators were arrested or tried.

Brewer, Richard

Considered by some to be the only "white hat" in the whole Lincoln County War, Dick Brewer appeared to be widely respected throughout the county as a small rancher, then Tunstall's foreman, then deputy constable and leader of the Regulators until he was killed at Blazer's Mill by Buckshot Roberts. He was 28 at his death.

Bristol, Judge Warren
Associate Justice of NM Supreme Court and primary judicial authority in Lincoln County throughout the Lincoln County War. Bristol, as an associate of the Santa Fe Ring, was openly hostile to McSween and partisan to the Murphy-Dolan side. He presided at the trial of Billy the Kid and sentenced him to be "hanged by the neck until the body be dead."

Brown, Henry Newton
Although not a "major player" in Billy's life, Brown's ending is – ahem – interesting. Brown rode with the Regulators and participated in the attack on Sheriff Brady, the Blazer's Mill shootout, and the "Five Days Battle" that ended with the burning of the McSween house. Brown left New Mexico, became marshal of Caldwell, Kansas and built an impressive reputation capped by being awarded a gold and silver mounted Winchester. But, all good things must end. Telling the mayor they were off to hunt a murderer, Brown with two cowboys tried to hold up the bank in Medicine Lodge, failed and fled, were trapped in a box canyon, eventually killed by a lynch mob. Not the sharpest knife in the rack, Brown had neglected to remove his marshal's badge before the holdup.

Catron, Thomas
U.S. Attorney and leader of the Santa Fe Ring, which was accused of illegal and bullying tactics to acquire land. Catron, with his law partner Stephen Elkins, gained controlling interest in the First National Bank of Santa Fe and eventually amassed three million acres making him one of the largest landowners in the U.S. Catron sided with Murphy and Dolan throughout the Lincoln County War, later was U.S. Senator.

Chapman, Huston

Lawyer who represented Susan McSween following her husband's death in the last battle of the Lincoln County War. Chapman aggressively pressed her case against Fort Stanton commander Lieutenant Colonel Dudley, charging him with responsibility in the death of Alexander McSween.

On the evening of February 18, 1879, a "peace parley" was held between Billy the Kid and the Dolan faction; afterwards the participants repaired to a saloon, soon becoming raucous. Outside they encountered Chapman and demanded that he dance. Upon his refusal Chapman was shot in cold blood, evidently by Dolan cohort Billy Campbell.

The Chapman murder was witnessed by Billy the Kid, and subsequently Governor Wallace made a promise to him that, if Billy would testify against the killers, Wallace would see that indictments against Billy would be dropped (Wallace, years later, said he promised Billy a pardon). Billy kept his side of the bargain, Wallace reneged.

Chisum, John

One of the first to appreciate the opportunities for cattle-raising on open ranges in southeastern New Mexico, Chisum drove a herd of several hundred from Texas that eventually grew to over 100,000 head. In that wide-open and essentially lawless country where rustling and brand alteration were common, Chisum created a non-alterable brand: the "jingle-bob" formed by a slit in the cow's ear such that a part flopped over. His pressure on smaller cattlemen created animosities that flowered during the Lincoln County War, although the war was primarily about business monopoly and not cattle. Chisum was aligned with newcomers Tunstall and McSween in establishing a bank and mercantile in Lincoln to compete directly with the Murphy-Dolan store. Intolerant of competition, Dolan had Tunstall murdered and, as they would say then, "the ball was begun." Not the fellow with the cattle trail named after him – that was Jesse Chisholm.

Coe, Frank & George

Cousins and farmers who fought as Regulators on the McSween side in the Lincoln County War. Both survived. In 1898 Frank Coe shotgunned the man his daughter was fixing to elope with; he was acquitted, presumably with the usual claim of self-defense.

Dolan, James

A pugnacious Irishman who did not accept the notion of a free enterprise, competitive economic system, preferring instead to, literally, kill his competition. Indicted for Tunstall murder but friendship with Santa Fe Ring led to the case being dropped.

Though also charged in the murder of Chapman (see Huston Chapman entry above), Dolan's defense was typical for him: he claimed to have been very drunk and knew nothing. The description by the *Mesilla Valley Independent* and quoted in Frederick Nolan's *The Lincoln County War* bears repeating:

He saw nothing, neither did he know anything about the shooting of Chapman; he did not see Chapman shot and did not know that he was killed until after his arrival at the hotel. He acknowledged that he fired a shot, but stated that he fired it "to attract the attention of the party" – to call the boys off. Heard Evans talking, but did not know who he was talking to. In short, Mr. Dolan knew nothing about the killing of Chapman, although he was not ten feet away.

It will be remembered by those who read the newspapers that Mr. Dolan once denied over his own signature that he was present when Chapman was killed. He afterwards admitted that he was present but unarmed. He now admits that he was present and he was armed, and he fired the first shot but that he fired it to attract the attention of the party. He stood in the midst of a party of eight or ten men and had to fire his pistol in order to attract their attention!

Soon leaving Mesilla, Dolan headed back to Lincoln County for his forthcoming wedding. He was later elected county Treasurer and then to the Territorial Senate. In an act of extreme irony, he purchased all of Tunstall's property. Died February 6, 1898, apparently from alcohol poisoning.

Dudley, Lt. Colonel Nathan
Characterized as tyrannical, egomaniacal, antagonistic, condescending, bombastic, and defiant, Dudley used the forces of the U.S. Army to assist the Murphy-Dolan faction in the Lincoln County War, and can probably be proximately blamed for the death of several men including Alexander McSween. He was thrice court-martialed and found guilty, but because of "friends in high places" he was able to continue in service until his retirement in 1889.

Evans, Jesse
One of the two (with John Kinney) most active and vicious outlaws in New Mexico Territory, brought in or at least welcomed in Lincoln County to fight on the Murphy-Dolan side, along with a variable number of cohort outlaws from Texas and southern New Mexico. In the "posse" that ran down and murdered Tunstall, and in the group that murdered Chapman. Eventually on the run from Lincoln, Texas Rangers caught up with his band near Presidio del Norte, in Mexico. In the ensuing gun battle, Evans shot and killed Ranger George Bingham. Arrested, tried, sentenced to prison, escaped, recaptured, sent to Huntsville Prison. Released in 1882 and was never seen or heard from again. Never really brought to justice.

Fritz family
Emil Fritz was Lawrence Murphy's partner and an associate of the notorious Santa Fe Ring that virtually ruled the New Mexico Territory in the late 1800s. When Fritz died, Alexander McSween was engaged to obtain the proceeds of an insurance policy on his life. Complications arose and Fritz's heirs, encouraged by James Dolan, filed suit against McSween for embezzlement. A grand jury exonerated McSween shortly before he was killed in the final battle of the Lincoln County War.

Garrett, Pat

After shooting Billy in 1881, Garrett became a Texas Ranger, rancher, then sheriff of Doña Ana County, appointed Collector of Customs at El Paso but President Theodore Roosevelt refused to reappoint him. Disappointed, Garrett went back to ranching, and was killed in 1908 under "questionable" circumstances.

Kinney, John

One of the more notorious New Mexico outlaws in the 1870s and 80s, John Kinney engaged in cattle rustling, robbery, and occasional killings. Along with Jesse Evans and other known outlaws, he was recruited into the Murphy-Dolan faction during the Lincoln County War. Kinney survived a shot to the face by Billy the Kid during the final battle in Lincoln, served a couple of years in prison for rustling, and died in Prescott, Arizona in his seventies.

House, the

Before Tunstall, McSween, and Chisum opened a competing mercantile store and bank, Lincoln was essentially a company town, with virtually all business going through "the House," the Murphy-Dolan store and peripheral enterprises. The House, with ample influence in the Santa Fe Ring, controlled the lucrative contracts to furnish beef to the Army forts and Indian agencies, buying cheaply from local ranchers and farmers. It then charged these same suppliers exorbitantly for their clothing, utensils, tools, flour, coffee and other "necessaries." The House was powerful, but also powerfully unpopular.

McCarty, Catherine

Billy's mother, to whom he was devoted during her life and always afterward. Reportedly a stalwart worker and citizen during her life, she died of tuberculosis, consumption it was called then, in 1874. Speculation has it that she emigrated from Ireland, but no conclusive evidence has been found.

McSween, Alexander

Lawyer who, when first arriving in Lincoln, did some work for Murphy-Dolan, then when Emil Fritz died was engaged to recover insurance proceeds. Soon McSween became associated with John Tunstall in opening a competing store and bank. Angered, the Murphy-Dolan combine persuaded the Fritz family to bring charges of embezzlement against McSween. He was exonerated by the grand jury shortly before being killed at the age of 25 in what was essentially the final battle of the Lincoln County War.

McSween, Susan

Widowed, she deftly administered the estates of her slain lawyer husband and John Tunstall, his English partner; brought lawsuits and countersuits; weathered threats against her life and a scandal; purchased land, made improvements, and sold properties; divorced her second husband; slowly but shrewdly built and managed a cattle empire and was later dubbed the Cattle Queen of New Mexico. Succeeded in a man's world and lived out her independent, self-empowered life long enough to see – then scold and walk out on – King Vidor's 1930 film, "Billy The Kid," in Carrizozo's Lyric Theater just six weeks before her death.

Maxwell, Deluvina

Born Navajo in 1851, taken as a child in an Apache raid, subsequently traded to Lucien Maxwell for horses. She stayed with the Maxwells at Fort Sumner after Lucien died. Since Billy the Kid frequented Fort Sumner and was friends with the Maxwells (possibly *more* than friends with Paulita Maxwell), Deluvina became acquainted with Billy and developed a great fondness for him.

Maxwell, Paulita

Paulita, 17 years old when Garrett shot Billy, was Pete Maxwell's sister and the daughter of New Mexico land baron Lucien Maxwell. She may have been Billy the Kid's lover, although in later years, after she had been married and given birth to three children, Paulita only admitted to having been very fond of him.

Maxwell, Pedro ("Pete")

Son of New Mexico land baron Lucien Maxwell and brother of Paulita, Pete Maxwell was a leading citizen of Fort Sumner and a friend of Billy the Kid's. He was 33 years old when Garrett shot Billy the Kid in Pete's bedroom on July 14, 1881.

Murphy, Lawrence

Union Army veteran of the Civil War, Murphy used his military contacts to secure contracts to supply Army posts and Indian agencies with meat and produce. Eventually his store in Lincoln enjoyed a virtual monopoly. After first partner Emil Fritz died Murphy joined with James Dolan and, supported by the Santa Fe Ring, soon held economic and political sway over most of Lincoln County. The Lincoln County War, triggered largely by the murder of John Tunstall, was also fueled by smoldering animosity toward Murphy and Dolan for their store's harsh terms, as well as for their reputation for shady land deals and paying bounties for rustled cattle (primarily John Chisum's).

Tom O'Folliard

A Texan, Tom was close to Billy's age and came to New Mexico in the late months of the Lincoln County War. He quickly got involved with the Regulators and became Billy's best friend. Tom was shot and killed in December, 1880, by Garrett's posse that was lying in ambush as Billy and several of his friends came riding into Fort Sumner.

Olinger, Bob

Big Bob Olinger was an outlaw and killer long before Pat Garrett appointed him a deputy, first to help escort Billy the Kid to trial in Mesilla and from there to jail in Lincoln, and then with James Bell to guard Billy until the date set for his hanging. Olinger manifested a deep and continuous animosity toward Billy, possibly because Billy was never cowed by Olinger's bullying and blustering ways. Olinger was killed by a shot, purportedly from his own shotgun, by Billy as he made his escape from Lincoln in April, 1881.

Riley, John

Irishman Riley became a partner in "the House" with James Dolan after Lawrence Murphy's death. He participated in the Lincoln County War on the Dolan side, of course, and afterward moved to Las Cruces. He eventually ended up a hog farmer in Colorado.

Roberts, Andrew "Buckshot"

Prior to coming to New Mexico Roberts was said to have been involved in a shootout with Texas Rangers that left him with a load of buckshot in his right shoulder, preventing him from raising his right arm. Roberts was in the "posse" that ran down and killed John Tunstall, so naturally he chose the Dolan side in that war. In April 1878 he wandered into Blazer's Mill not knowing that the Regulators were already there and holding a warrant for Roberts' arrest. Refusing to surrender, Roberts kicked off a shootout that ended with Roberts and Regulator leader Dick Brewer dead, and several Regulators wounded. Despite his injured right shoulder, Roberts was later characterized as "one hell of a shot" with a rifle held only waist-high.

Rynerson, Dist. Attorney William

Associate of the Santa Fe Ring and killer of New Mexico Chief Justice John P. Slough (he got off on the time-honored claim of self-defense), good friend of L. G. Murphy, J. J. Dolan, and J. H. Riley and helped them all he could in the Lincoln County War. Before the war, he lent Dolan the money he needed to buy a partnership in L. G. Murphy & Co. Rynerson also wrote a letter to Dolan and Riley advising them to simply kill John Tunstall. Towards the end of the war, Rynerson hired the John Kinney gang (who roamed Doña Ana County) and sent them to Lincoln County to serve as more gunmen for Dolan. After the war, he was "prosecuting attorney" in Dolan's trial for murder, so the charges against Dolan were quickly dropped. It was also primarily because of Rynerson that Billy Bonney never received the pardon promised him by Gov. Lew Wallace. In order for Billy to have received the pardon, the prosecuting attorney (Rynerson) would have to agree to it, and Rynerson intended to prosecute Billy fully. Rynerson later partnered with Dolan and others to establish a ranch on Tunstall's old property, called the Feliz Land & Cattle Co. He died on September 26, 1893.

Scurlock, Josiah "Doc"

Trained in medicine, Scurlock was one of Billy the Kid's first friends in New Mexico. He fought on the side of the Regulators in the Lincoln County War, eventually becoming their leader. After surviving several close scrapes Scurlock left for Texas, became a teacher, and died in 1929.

Tunstall, John

Englishman Tunstall came to New Mexico looking for investment opportunities, soon set up a small ranch (and hired William Bonney, among others). Seeing that the Murphy-Dolan store had a virtual monopoly in Lincoln and thereby controlled the beef contracts with the Army and the Indian agencies, Tunstall opened a competing store and bank with Alexander McSween and John Chisum as co-investors (they were never legally partners before Tunstall died). At the age of 24, in February 1878, Tunstall was murdered by a "posse" sent by Sheriff Brady and incited by James Dolan. His murder triggered the Lincoln County War, resulting in protests from the British government which in turn led to an extensive investigation by federal agent Angel.

Wallace, Governor Lew

Union Civil War general, appointed governor of New Mexico Territory in 1878. To reduce violence Wallace offered amnesty to virtually all Lincoln County War participants unless they were already under indictment. Ultimately that exception applied only to Billy the Kid.

Wallace promised Billy a pardon if Billy would testify as to the murderers of Chapman. Billy did so even though it meant the actual killers would come gunning for him, but Wallace reneged on his commitment. Billy was therefore prosecuted, convicted, sentenced to hang, killed two guards to escape, and was shot by Garrett in Fort Sumner – all fruits of Wallace's perfidy. But Wallace apparently never looked back, basking as he was in the success of *Ben Hur: A Tale of The Christ.* Wallace resigned as governor in March 1881 to become U.S. Minister to the Ottoman Empire; on the day Billy was shot in New Mexico, Wallace and his wife were in Paris enjoying the nighttime fireworks celebrating Bastille Day.

Widenmann, Robert

Widenmann was one of the men riding with John Tunstall the day Tunstall was killed. Using his father's connections Widenmann got himself appointed a deputy U.S. Marshall. He supported the posse of Regulators that included Billy the Kid in seeking to find and arrest Tunstall's killers. These appointments were later cancelled by Territorial Governor Axtell. Widenmann lived until 1930.

Significant Places
(In New Mexico, unless otherwise noted)

Anton Chico: Village 20 miles south of Las Vegas, 80 miles north of Fort Sumner, between today's I-25 and I-40. One of Billy the Kid's favorite haunts (and markets for stolen stock) after the Lincoln County War, where he could often be found dealing monte and dancing at the *bailes*. Not-yet-sheriff Pat Garrett married his 17-year-old second wife in Anton Chico.

Blazer's Mill: Sawmill owned by Dr. Joseph Blazer, roughly between today's Ruidoso and Tularosa; part of the property was leased to the U.S. government for the Mescalero Indian agency. Scene of a gun battle in April 1878 between the Regulators and "Buckshot" Roberts that left Regulator leader Dick Brewer and Roberts dead, others wounded.

Fort Grant: Army fort in southeastern Arizona where Billy the Kid went after leaving Silver City, and the site of his first killing in an altercation with local bully and blacksmith "Windy" Cahill.

Fort Stanton: Small Army fort a dozen miles west of Lincoln, New Mexico. Civilian authorities called for assistance from troops at Fort Stanton to curtail outlaw activity and eventually to end the Lincoln County War. Black calvary troops, often referred to as "Buffalo soldiers," were quartered there.

Fort Sumner: Army post on the Pecos River created in 1862, site of the Bosque Redondo reservation to which some 9,000 Navajo and Apache Indians were removed in the early 1860s. (Alkaline water, crop failure, much illness and deaths eventually led the U.S. government to allow the Navajos to return to their homeland; the Apaches had already simply walked away.) The fort's buildings and property were acquired by Lucien Maxwell after it was abandoned by the army. Fort Sumner was one of Billy the Kid's favorite haunts, as well as the home of more than one rumored sweetheart. On the evening of July 14, 1881, Billy the Kid was shot by Pat Garrett as

Billy backed into Pete Maxwell's Fort Sumner bedroom. Garrett had been quietly questioning Maxwell there in the dark about Billy's location. Fort Sumner is now a small town and the site of the Bosque Redondo State Monument, as well as the purported grave of Billy the Kid.

La Mesilla: Village in southern New Mexico, now a suburb of Las Cruces, which was an important site in the early history of the state and particularly during the Lincoln County War. Outlaws such as John Kinney were recruited from Mesilla to fight for the Dolan side the war. Site of Billy the Kid's trial and conviction for murder of Sheriff Brady in 1881.

Las Vegas: Most important commercial center in New Mexico Territory, and largest city between St. Louis and San Francisco, during Billy the Kid's days. Billy passed through Las Vegas after his surrender to Pat Garrett in December, 1880, on his way to jail in Santa Fe and subsequent trial in La Mesilla. In 1848 General Stephen Kearny, leading the U.S. Army of the West, had marched into Las Vegas and, from a perch overlooking the plaza, declared New Mexico to henceforth be part of the United States.

Lincoln: Village on the Rio Bonito in southeastern New Mexico, now a state monument but in the 1870s the center of the Lincoln County War. Lincoln was the locus of much of Billy the Kid's life from the time he returned to New Mexico in 1877 until he was shot (at Fort Sumner) by Pat Garrett in 1881. The village today looks much as it did in 1878 after the McSween house was burned.

Mesilla (see La Mesilla)

Puerto de Luna: Ancient village on the Pecos River ten miles south of Santa Rosa, popular with Billy the Kid and friends for its *bailes* and as a market for stolen livestock. After his capture by Garrett just before Christmas 1880, Billy and his compadres were taken by wagon to Puerto de Luna where they were served Christmas dinner at Grzelachowski's ranch, on their way to the Las Vegas.

Roswell: Town some 50 miles east of Lincoln, north of the Seven Rivers area and south of Fort Sumner, near the Pecos River. Not especially significant during the Lincoln County War but as a crossroads would have seen many of the participants, and of course became famous for another reason 70 years later. John Chisum's

Jingle Bob (sometimes JingleBob, Jinglebob) Ranch was nearby.

San Patricio: A favorite haunt of Billy the Kid and other Regulators during and after the Lincoln County War. Just southeast "over the hill" from Lincoln, San Patricio was far enough away to afford Billy and friends ample time to skedaddle should word reach them that a posse was heading their way. Today San Patricio is not nearly as lively as it was in 1878.

Seven Rivers: Area in southeastern New Mexico where seven creeks flowed into the Pecos River. Small ranchers, antagonized by the intrusiveness of Chisum's huge cattle empire, engaged in continuous rustling of Chisum's cattle, encouraged by a bounty per head offered by Dolan. The area became something of a magnet and sanctuary for Texas outlaws drawn to the violence in Lincoln County.

Silver City: Mining town in southwestern New Mexico which, in the 1870s, attracted Catherine McCarty, Billy the Kid's mother, and her husband William Antrim. They came in the hope that the warm dry climate would heal her consumption, or tuberculosis. Catherine established a respected laundry but the disease overtook her. She died in Silver City September 16, 1874. Billy attended school in Silver City while living there.

Stinking Springs: An old forage station east of Fort Sumner where Billy the Kid and three companions were captured by Pat Garrett's posse in December, 1880 (a fourth, Charlie Bowdre, was killed by Garrett's posse earlier in the day). The name apparently came from the odor of decaying vegetation nearby.

Tascosa, Texas (usually Old Tascosa today): Ghost town northwest of Amarillo that was thriving during the days of Billy the Kid. Saloons catered to the cowboys of the nearby XIT and other ranches as well as to herd-driving trail hands. Tascosa was the perfect market for horses and cattle that Billy and his friends would drive up from Lincoln County.

White Oaks: Mining town some 25-30 miles northwest of Lincoln. Its population of several hundred supported saloons, general stores, brothels, and a school. It was one of Billy the Kid's favorite towns especially when things got too hot in Lincoln, and was always a dependable market for stolen livestock.

Wichita, Kansas: Town on the Arkansas River in south central

Kansas that was home in the early 1870s to Billy the Kid (then Henry McCarty), brother Josie, his mother Catherine McCarty, and Catherine's friend William Antrim (they were subsequently married in Santa Fe). As she did later in Silver City, Catherine operated a respected laundry in downtown Wichita. She also homesteaded property northeast of town and was the only woman to sign Wichita's incorporation petition.

The Lincoln County War, in short

Lincoln County, today a place unfamiliar to most Americans, was much in their focus during the 1870s. Established in 1869, it was enlarged in 1878 to encompass most of the southeast quarter of New Mexico Territory, running roughly 160 miles wide and 180 miles long.

Early on there was a small settlement called Placitas on the pretty Rio Bonito (that adjective is redundant, of course). It was soon renamed Bonito, then changed by the legislature to Lincoln in honor of the late president.

During the height of the Lincoln County War, the single road through town was described as "the most dangerous street in America." Because of its historical significance the town of Lincoln has been preserved as a New Mexico State Monument, and looks today much as it did in 1878.

A few Texas cattle were driven to southeastern New Mexico ranges in the 1860s, hundreds of thousands followed in the 1870s – attracted by good grazing on unsurveyed public domain, and a growing demand for beef from the Indian agencies and army forts. The area was essentially unpoliced, unorganized, and ungoverned; easy pickings fostered hundreds of cattle thieves.

The future of Lincoln was foreshadowed in 1873 by what came to be called the Harrell War. The Harrells had decamped to the Ruidoso River from Texas after killing four state police. Several were whooping it up in Lincoln when the constable called on them to turn over their guns. In the ensuing battle the constable plus three of the Harrells gang were killed.

A few weeks later the revenge-minded Harrells along with a number of cohorts rode back into Lincoln and shot up a *baile,* a dance and fiesta, killing four Mexicans. Subsequently the sheriff and a large posse surrounded the gang in an old adobe. Many bullets were fired, no one got hurt, and the Harrells headed back to Texas.

A mass meeting to deal with the disorders was run by Lawrence Murphy and James Dolan, laying the foundation for their dominance of the region. Murphy, William Brady, and Jose Montano were designated to take "all necessary action."

For perhaps the first but certainly not the last time the territorial governor, Marsh Giddings, appealed to the president for military assistance. (Samuel Axtell, who "presided" during much of the period of the Lincoln County War, succeeded Giddings in 1875.)

Soon Murphy's store was the scene of a killing, a harbinger of things to come. The store clerk and a deputy sheriff got into an argument, shot it out, the deputy was killed and the clerk got off.

Blood continued to run hot. Robert Casey was ambushed and killed by William Wilson, after Casey verbally attacked the Murphy organization at a political convention. Wilson was tried and hanged – for 9 and a half minutes, then put in a coffin but found to be still alive, henceforth taken out and hung for 20 minutes more.

In 1876 rustlers tried to lift five horses from some tough fellows who later formed part of the core of the Regulators. Frank Coe, Ab Saunders, Doc Scurlock, Charlie Bowdre, plus some neighboring farmers, in short order captured and shot or lynched the three gang leaders.

Another horse thief, Jose Segura, was being transported to nearby Fort Stanton guarded by the sheriff and three men, when seventeen masked men overpowered them, wrested Segura away, and shot him.

John Chisum's "cattle kingdom" was bound to be a magnet for rustlers, especially when they were offered a bounty by James Dolan. Chisum apparently riled Frank Freeman, an abusive racist who ran to Texas after murdering a black soldier from Fort Stanton. Freeman was soon back in Lincoln, got drunk, shot another soldier in the back, then went looking for Chisum.

Freeman fired a barrage of shots at Alexander McSween's house where Chisum was visiting. Wounded by a servant, Freeman retreated to the Murphy-Dolan store and was eventually arrested by Sheriff Brady – after a scuffle in which Brady floored Freeman and Freeman then flattened Brady. Freeman later escaped from a military escort while being taken to Fort Stanton.

An ally of Freeman, one Armstrong, got liquored up in Lincoln and started shooting indiscriminately. He was chased and killed by a posse. The sheriff and posse then went after Freeman; Freeman shot at the posse, the posse killed Freeman.

Such violence is sure to attract a bad crowd, like buzzards to carrion. Jesse Evans was known as a major horse and cattle thief in the Mesilla Valley, but that area became too hot for him after he ambushed Quinino Fletcher in revenge. In Lincoln County he buddied up with Murphy's partner James Dolan and was soon identified as the leader of a gang called "the Boys."

Killing was the almost-accepted way to settle most any quarrel – probably considered the "manly" way. The killing of Hilario Jaramillo in 1877 by James Dolan is illustrative. Dolan killed Jaramillo in cold blood, or in anger because Jaramillo had warned Dolan's friend George Peppin to stay away from Jaramillo's wife, or because Jaramillo fought him off when Dolan made "unnatural advances" toward him. At least one of the above.

Soon guns were the main arbiter of quarrels in Lincoln County. In May 1877, Capt. Paul Dowlin was shot and killed, though unarmed, by Jerry Dillon. Witnesses say Dillon fired twice at Dowlin with a carbine, then shot him with a revolver, while Dowlin all the while attempted to reason with Dillon. Dillon lit out for Texas and was never heard from again.

The violence in Lincoln County, sometimes appearing to be random and unrelated, was building an environment flashing with animosity, hatred, anger, lust for revenge. Sides were forming, Murphy-Dolan and the Santa Fe Ring on one side, the small farmers, ranchers, shopkeepers and most native New Mexicans – or simply Mexicans as they were usually identified – on the other. In April 1877 an ailing Murphy decided to sell out, and the store now became James J. Dolan and Co. (with another Irishman, John H. Riley, added as partner). The company was commonly referred to as "the House."

By December, Dolan was able to fan into flames a complicated – and small – legal conflict.

Lawyer Alexander McSween had been working to obtain the proceeds from a life insurance policy following the death of Emil Fritz; the process was time-consuming and convoluted. Dolan was encouraging the Fritz family to make an embezzlement claim against

McSween, and Judge Bristol then issued a warrant for McSween's arrest. McSween and John Chisum, traveling together through Las Vegas, were coarsely arrested, with some physical abuse (Chisum on unrelated charges growing out of a complicated financial deal).

John Tunstall was a young Englishman who, after becoming acquainted with McSween in Santa Fe, decided to accompany him to Lincoln County where he soon bought a ranch on the Rio Felix. A few months later, with support from McSween and Chisum, Tunstall began mercantile and banking operation in Lincoln in direct competition with "the House." Dolan evidently saw the battle lines as now drawn clearly.

Tunstall soon earned a reputation as an honest businessman who would pay a fair price for the farmers' crops and not gouge with his mercantile prices. But he was apparently naive about the ways of Lincoln County, and the prevailing culture of resolving conflicts with a gun. On January 18, 1878, he published an accusatory letter in the Mesilla *Independent*. In it he charged Sheriff Brady with misappropriating $1,500 of Lincoln County tax collections and passing the money to J. J. Dolan & Co.

A couple of weeks later McSween weighed in with a letter to U.S. Interior Secretary Schurz, accusing Dolan & Co. of providing unfit beef and spoiled flour to the Mescalero Indian agency, stealing back supplies from the agency and reselling them, and engaging in widespread cattle theft.

The hostility of Dolan, Brady, and cohorts was starting to boil. The fire was further stoked by a letter from District Attorney Rynerson addressed to "Friends of Riley & Dolan." Referring to Tunstall and McSween, Rynerson wrote [spelling from original]:

I believe Tunstall is in with the swindles with the rogue McSween. They have the money belonging to the Fritz estate and they must be made to give it up. It must be made hot for them all the hotter the better especially is this necessary now that it has been discovered that there is no hell. It may be that the villian Green "Juan Bautista" Wilson will play into their hands as Alcalde. If so he should be moved around a little. Shake that McSween outfit up till it shells out and squares up and then shake

it out of Lincoln. I will aid to punish the
scoundrels all I can. Get the people with you.
Control Juan Patrón if possible. You know how to do
it. Have good men about to aid Brady and be assured
I shall help you all I can for I believe there was
never found a more scoundrely set than that outfit.

Brady then levied an attachment against McSween's assets in the
town of Lincoln and, on the untrue claim that Tunstall was
McSween's legal partner, on Tunstall's as well. He followed up by
sending a posse to attach Tunstall's ranch and livestock. Figuring on
resolving things in court Tunstall decided against opposing the
attachment, and set out for Lincoln accompanied by Richard Brewer,
Robert Widenmann, John Middleton, and William Bonney.

Part of Brady's posse, now including known and wanted outlaws,
caught up with Tunstall while he was separated from his protectors by
a few hundred yards, and killed him in cold blood. The coroner's jury
concluded:

We . . . find that the deceased came to his
death on the 18th day of February A.D., 1878, by
means of divers bullets shot and sent forth out of
and from deadly weapons, and upon the head and body
of the said John H. Tunstall, which said deadly
weapons then and there were held by one or more of
the men whose names are herewith written: Jesse
Evans, Frank Baker, Thomas Hill, George Hindman, J.
J. Dolan, William Morton, and others not identified
by witnesses that testified before the coroner's
jury.

(Subsequent testimony and evidence indicate that the actual
killers were Evans, Hill, and Morton.)

Despite claims by members of the so-called posse that they were
acting only in self-defense because Tunstall was resisting arrest and
had fired at them first, evidence and testimony revealed that Tunstall
did not fire a shot, but was first shot through the breast with a rifle
and then in the back of the head with a revolver. Next the gang
removed Tunstall's holstered pistol and discharged it into the air to
support the claim that they had been fired upon. Apparently motivated
by intent to demean and humiliate, they then shot Tunstall's horse,

placed Tunstall's hat under the horse's head, and placed a folded overcoat under Tunstall's head – creating an image of "two figures in sweet repose."

Presumably concerned by how all this was going to reflect on him personally, Brady sent a letter two weeks later inclosing a note to deputy sheriff Matthews (which he claimed he had written on February 15th, before the Tunstall killing) containing the following instructions: "Dear Sir: You must not by any means call on or allow to travel with your posse any person or persons who are known to be outlaws." In the eyes of the public this effort seems to have backfired on Brady, appearing so obviously to be an after-the-fact effort to cover his rear.

Justice of the Peace Wilson issued a warrant for arrest of the murderers, as well as a warrant for the arrest of Sheriff Brady on a somewhat trivial complaint of larceny by McSween. Constable Atanacio Martinez, fearing for his life, was unwilling to serve the warrants alone. William Bonney and Fred Waite promised to back him up, and the three of them marched to the Dolan store where they were met by Brady and others with drawn guns.

Brady not only refused to be arrested but instead threw the three in jail. The next day a meeting of citizens decried the action of Brady in arresting, without warrant, a legally empowered constable and his deputies who were themselves carrying valid arrest warrants. Brady's response was sneering dismissal. But soon thereafter Deputy U.S. Marshal Widenmann, backed up by a military escort, marched Brady before Wilson where he was made to post bond on the larceny charge.

Despite this small victory McSween feared for his life. The animus of Dolan and "the Boys" was surely directed at him as much as at Tunstall. He made out a will leaving everything to his wife, and headed for the hills.

Outraged over the murder of Tunstall, Dick Brewer had Wilson appoint him a deputy constable; he then organized a posse of Tunstall cowboys and other supporters to go after the killers. They called themselves Regulators, an honorable label from American history for citizens seeking to enforce law and order in the face of established authorities that had become crooked or venal.

The Regulators headed down the Pecos River and soon caught

and arrested Morton and Baker. The next day, while passing through Blackwater Canyon, Morton, Baker, and William McCloskey were killed. The story told was that Baker grabbed McCloskey's pistol and shot him, then Baker and Morton made a run for it and were quickly killed. "Shot while trying to escape" seemed to vie with "self-defense" as the prime cause of death throughout the old West.

Soon thereafter Evans and Hill, in an incident unrelated to the growing conflict in Lincoln, raided a sheep drover's camp and shot the Cherokee tending the camp. But the Cherokee wasn't killed. He grabbed a rifle, killed Hill, and put a bullet through Jesse Evans' elbow. Evans escaped and made it to the Post Hospital at Fort Stanton, where Widenmann caught up with him and served him with a warrant. Evans was soon transferred to the guardhouse and eventually got out on bond, in time to participate in the "Five Days Battle" (see below).

Meanwhile McSween, camping around in the hills and waiting for court to convene so he could appear and clear his name, was persuaded by an Army lieutenant to come into the protection of the fort. McSween and company got delayed by heavy rains, fell behind the military escort, and never caught up. They were on their way into Lincoln, without protection, on the morning of April 1st 1878.

Several of the Regulators had already arrived in Lincoln, whether to await the court or to serve as protection for McSween is unknown. Possibly they believed Brady and crew were aiming to kill McSween when he appeared in town. Possibly they viewed Brady as the commanding general of a rogue army, responsible in that capacity for Tunstall's death and much of the other killing and brigandage. Possibly they acted simply out of revenge or anger. Whatever the motivation, as Brady and four deputies, all heavily armed, passed in front of the Tunstall store a hail of bullets brought him and deputy George Hindman down. Whether William Bonney ever shot at or hit Brady (Garrett thought he hadn't), he was present and was subsequently the only one tried for the murder.

The Regulators rode out of Lincoln and, under the leadership of Dick Brewer, now went searching for men for whom Brewer held warrants. They stopped at Blazer's Mill, and in a short while a heavily-armed Andrew Roberts, known as "Buckshot" and a member of the so-called posse that murdered Tunstall, rode up. Frank Coe went out to meet Roberts and, saying they had a warrant for him, asked him to surrender. Roberts refused, a lengthy gun battle ensured, both Brewer and Roberts were killed, George Coe and John Middleton were wounded. Bonney later said Roberts "licked our crowd to a finish."

In April a grand jury met and was treated to highly biased and splenetic instructions from Judge Bristol – he spent pages maligning McSween and only a couple of sentences on the Tunstall murder. Nevertheless, the grand jury completely exonerated McSween. It returned indictments against Jesse Evans and three others for the murder of Tunstall with Dolan and Mathews as accessories. It indicted four Regulators including Bonney (as Henry Antrim or "Kidd") for murder of Brady and Hindman, and nine Regulators for the "murder" of Roberts. Finally, Dolan and Riley were indicted for cattle theft.

With Brewer dead Frank MacNab took over leadership of the Regulators. Meanwhile a large gang of outlaws from the Seven Rivers area down south was now in league with Dolan and roaming Lincoln County seeking Regulators to kill. They surprised MacNab, Ab Saunders, and Frank Coe while watering their horses, killed MacNab, seriously wounded Saunders, and captured Coe. When the gang rode into Lincoln with Coe in tow, Regulators were already there and a gun battle ensued that lasted until an army detachment rode in and broke it up.

For several weeks sporadic gun battles and legal maneuverings occurred. A flood of letters complaining about conditions in Lincoln County were addressed to President Hayes, members of Congress, and the U.S. Attorney General and Secretary of the Interior. These finally took effect. A special agent was appointed, New York lawyer Frank Warner Angel, to go to Lincoln, investigate the situation, and report back.

Angel promptly set about taking affidavits from virtually all the figures in the Lincoln County War. Though his reports were months away, rumors began to circulate that he was going to be much more critical of the Dolan than the McSween side, and that territorial executives including Governor Axtell and U.S. Attorney Catron were likely to be replaced.

Meanwhile McSween, knowing he was still a marked man and fearing for his life, had once again taken to the hills. But in July, possibly encouraged by Angel's presence and the possibility of a breakup of the Santa Fe Ring, he reached a momentous decision: he was through hiding, he was going back to his home in Lincoln, and if Dolan or the Fritz family had a beef they could settle it in court.

The Regulators were alarmed; they were certain he would be murdered. So they rode into Lincoln ahead of McSween and took up positions in strategic locations throughout the town. Dolan's crew, although reinforced by the arrival of Jesse Evans, was badly outnumbered. Sheriff George Peppin, a through and through Dolan man, quickly sent for reinforcements from one of the vilest outlaws in the west, John Kinney and his gang.

Still the Regulators were dominant. Dolan and Peppin sent repeated appeals to Fort Stanton for assistance but Colonel Dudley, in command there, was constrained by his prior orders to not get the military involved. As Dolan persisted Dudley, leaning on a claim that one of his men had been fired upon, relented and dispatched infantry and cavalry, equipped with a howitzer and Gatling gun. The howitzer was set up in the road in front of McSween's house. Now the Regulators could not fire at Dolan's men without risking hitting a soldier, which would produce an immediate blast from the howitzer. The Regulators initial advantage was wiped out; they were pinned down.

Then, under the willing eyes of the army, some of Dolan's men started fires around the McSween house. At first those inside could extinguish them, but eventually the ancient timbers caught and forced everyone into a single room in the rear. As the room filled with smoke, the Regulators faced no good choices: they felt that if they surrendered they would be killed in the process, if they fired at Dolan's men there was a high risk they would be blown to bits by the cannon, if they stayed they would suffocate or burn to death. They finally opted for what was allegedly a Bonney plan: wait until nearly dark, then Bonney and four others would make a break out the back to draw fire, and the rest could then try to sneak out through the fence.

It sort of worked. One of Billy's first group and four of the remaining group, including McSween, were killed; the others, including Bonney, escaped.

Despite these escapes, with the aid of outlaws and the army Dolan had won. The Lincoln County War was essentially over.

The surviving Regulators mostly disbanded, went home to their farms and ranches or drifted out of the territory. A few stayed with Bonney, surviving by rustling cattle. In December of 1880 Pat Garrett and his posse tracked down Billy's small band, killing two and capturing the rest. Billy was tried, convicted, and sentenced to hang – the only person indicted, prosecuted, tried and convicted from the Lincoln County War. As is well known, he escaped from jail at Lincoln and soon thereafter was shot by Garrett in Fort Sumner.

This did not end outlaw activity in Lincoln County. But it did mark the end of one of the bloodiest, most violent wars in the American West.

Ralph Estes

Frank Warner Angel Report
Department of Justice

In the Matter of the Cause and Circumstances of the Death of John H. Tunstall, a British Subject

To the Honorable Charles Devens, Attorney General

In compliance with your instructions to make careful inquiry into the cause and circumstances of the death of John H. Tunstall, a British Subject, and whether the death of said Tunstall was brought about through the lawless and corrupt conduct of United State officials in the Territory of New Mexico, and a report thereon.

I have the honor to submit the following report in relation to the premises.

First: - As to the cause of death of John H. Tunstall.

Mr. John H. Tunstall, by his straight-forward and honest business transactions with the people of Lincoln County, New Mexico, had almost overthrown a certain faction of said County who were plundering the people thereof. He had been instrumental in the arrest of certain notorious horse thieves. He had exposed embezzlement of persons who had control of the County, and who used their control for private gain. He had introduced honesty and square dealings in his business, and to the enmity of these persons, can be attributed the only cause of his death.

Second: As to the circumstances of his death.

An attachment had been obtained against the property of one Alexander A. McSween.

It was claimed that said Tunstall was McSween's partner.

The Sheriff in order to attach certain property, viz, stock and horses, alleged to belong to McSween and Tunstall sent his deputy to Tunstall's ranch to attach the same – when said

112

deputy visited said ranch and was informed that he could attach the stock and leave a person with it until the Courts could adjudicate to whom the stock belonged – he left without attaching said property, and immediately assembles a large posse among whom were the most desperate out-laws of the Territory. They again started for Tunstall's ranch, in the meantime Mr. Tunstall had been informed of the action of the Sheriff, and believing that the real purpose was to murder and not attach left his ranch, taking with him all the horses and started for Lincoln, the County seat.

Directly after Tunstall had left his ranch, the Deputy Sheriff and said posse arrived there, and finding that Tunstall had left with the horses, deputized W. Morton who selected eighteen men and started out ostensibly to capture the horses. After riding about thirty miles they came up to Tunstall and his party with the horses, and commenced firing on them – Immediately Tunstall and his party left the horses and attempted to escape – were pursued and Tunstall was killed some hundred yards or more from the horses.

Who shot Tunstall will never be known. But there is no doubt that Wm. S. Morton, Jesse Evans and Hill were the only persons present and saw the shooting and two of those persons murdered him. For Tunstall was shot in two places – in the head and breast. Of these persons Morton and Hill were afterwards killed, and the only survivor is Jesse Evans a notorious out-law, murderer and horse-thief. Of these persons Evans and Hill had been arrested at the instigation of Tunstall

They were at enmity with Tunstall, and enmity with them meant murder.

There was no object for following after Tunstall except to murder him, for they had the horses which they desired to attach before they commenced to pursue him and his party. These facts, together with the bitter feeling existing against Tunstall, by certain persons to whom he had become obnoxious, and the deputy allowing these notorious out-laws to accompany him lead me to the conclusion that John H. Tunstall was murdered in cold blood, and was not shot in attempting to resist *an officer of the law.*

 <u>Third</u>: Was the death of John H. Tunstall brought about by the lawless and corrupt action of United States officials -

 After diligent enquiry and examination of a great number of witnesses, I report that the death of John H. Tunstall was not brought about through the lawless and corrupt conduct of United State officials in the Territory of New Mexico.

 All of which is respectfully submitted.

Frank Warner Angel
Special Agent

Frank Warner Angel Report
Department of Justice

In the Matter of the Lincoln County Troubles To the Honorable Charles Devens, Attorney General

The history of Lincoln County has been one of bloodshed from the day of its organization.

These troubles have existed for years with occasional outbreaks, each one being more severe than the other.

L. G. Murphy & Co. had the monopoly of all business in the county, controlled Government contracts, and used their power to oppress and grind out all they could from the farmers, and force those who were opposed to leave the County.

This has resulted in the formation of two parties, one led by Murphy & Co., and the other by McSween (now dead). Both have done many things contrary to law, both violated the law. McSween, I firmly believe, acted conscientiously – Murphy & Co. for private gain and revenge.

Bands of desperate characters who are ever found on the frontier, particularly along the Texas border, who have no interest in Lincoln County, men who live by plunder, and who only flourish where they can evade the law, have naturally gravitated to one or the other of these parties, and are now in their pay, being hired for so much a day to fight their battles.

Gov. Axtel appoints Peppin, a leader of the Murphy & Co. faction, as Sheriff, he comes to Lincoln accompanied by John Kinney and his notorious band of out-laws and murderers as a body guard to assist him in upholding law and order (?). McSween then collects around himself an equally distinguished body. The County becomes the elysium for out-laws and murderers.

A battle is fought – for five days it rages – more desperate action than was seen in these unfortunate days, by both sides, is rarely witnessed. Both parties desire revenge, and they are now reorganizing, and collecting more desperate characters (if it were possible), than they previously had. Before I left Santa Fe, it was reported that there were two hundred armed men in the field.

Men are shot down, "on sight" because they belong to one or the other party, and the residents of the County have been forced to take one side or the other either from inclination or necessity. One day Murphy & Co., and his party of out-laws control the County – the next day McSween and his "out-fit" would be the masters.

When these men were not engaged in battle, and when the County seemingly was at peace, they were employed to steal cattle, either from the farmers or the indians – a ready market and no questions asked, was found in the persons who held government contracts. If the people protested, they were persecuted and driven out [of] the County.

This state of affairs would be carried to such an extent, that it would end in a fight and a war, similar to the one now being waged in the County.

During these years the law-abiding citizens, or those, who would be if they could, have been reduced to poverty by professional thieves, who have made the County their camping ground without the least fear of molestation.

The laws cannot be enforced, for the reason that if the Murphy party are in power then the law is all Murphy – and if the McSween party are in power then the law is all McSween.

The leaders of these parties have created a storm that they cannot control, and it has reached such proportions that the whole Territory cannot put it down. Lands go uncultivated; ranches are abandoned; merchants have closed their stores; citizens have left the homes they have occupied for years; business has ceased, and lawlessness and murder are the order of the day.

These out-laws who prowl the County with the avowed purpose of murder, who have no interests in the County or wrongs of their own to redress, no matter on which side they belong, should be hunted down and made to answer for their crimes.

The Territory has no militia, and the County being in the hands of these armed out-laws, the laws and mandates of the Courts cannot be enforced or respected, nor lives or property protected. It is impossible for even the Courts to be held.

I would respectfully refer to my report to the Interior Department on the charges against Governor Axtell as to the additional causes for the existing troubles in Lincoln County.

I would most respectfully recommend that such assistance be given the Governor of New Mexico that the laws may be enforced and respected, and life and property protected.

All of which respectfully submitted.

Washington, October 7*th*, 1878
Frank Warner Angel
Special Agent

Selected Books

Hundreds of books have been published about Billy the Kid and the Lincoln County War. These are some of the best.

- Frederick Nolan, *The West of Billy the Kid*, Univ. of Oklahoma Press, 1998

- Frederick Nolan, *The Lincoln County War: A Documentary History*, Univ. of Oklahoma Press, 1992

- Mark Lee Gardner, *To Hell on a Fast Horse: Billy the Kid, Pat Garrett, and the Epic Chase to Justice in the Old West*, William Morrow, 2010

- Michael Wallis, *Billy the Kid: The Endless Ride*, W.W. Norton, 2007

- Willard Ballow, *Billy the Kid: A Graphic History*, Owlhoot Trail Publishing, 1998

- Bob Boze Bell, *The Illustrated Life and Times of Billy the Kid* (2d. ed.), Tri Star/Boze Publications, 1996

- Jon Tuska, *Billy the Kid: His Life and Legend*, Greenwood Press, 1994

- Robert Utley, *Billy the Kid: A Short and Violent Life*, Univ. of Nebraska Press, 1989

- Maurice Fulton, *History of the Lincoln County War: A Classic Account of Billy the Kid*, edited by Robert Mullin, Univ. of Arizona Press, 1968

- William Keleher, *Violence in Lincoln County 1869-1881*, Univ. of New Mexico Press, 1957

And the worst:

- Pat Garrett, *The Authentic Life of Billy, the Kid, The Noted Desperado of the Southwest, Whose Deeds of Daring and Blood Made His Name a Terror in New Mexico, Arizona, and Northern Mexico* (substantially written by Ash Upson), New Mexican Printing and Publishing Co., 1882

Text of Following Letters

During our conversations as Billy lay dying, he mentioned several times his regret that he had often been characterized as illiterate. He said he thought he had been able to go far enough in school to learn to write reasonably well and with decent grammar. Schooling, and some supportive teachers in Wichita and Silver City, had also ignited a lifelong love of reading. Even when he was on the run and living in caves or on the prairie, Billy said he read everything he could get his hands on. He often borrowed books from folks who had put him up for a night or two, but regretted that circumstances had prevented him from being able to return all of these.

Because of Billy's expressed concern, I have reproduced the originals of a couple of letters from Billy to Governor Lew Wallace, along with Wallace's response in which he says "I have authority to exempt you from prosecution, if you will testify to what you say you know" (Wallace later, in an interview, asserted that he had promised Billy a *pardon*). To my eye it appears that Billy's grammar and penmanship were not significantly worse than those of Wallace's secretary.

To aid in reading the letters, their full texts are presented in the following pages.

– Ralph Estes

On March 13, 1879 Billy the Kid writes to Governor Lew Wallace for the first time.

To his Excellency the Governor,
General Lew Wallace

Dear Sir, I have heard that You will give one thousand $ dollars for my body which as I can understand it means alive as a witness. I know it is as a witness against those that murdered Mr. Chapman. if it was so as that I could appear at Court I could give the desired information, but I have indictments against me for things that happened in the late Lincoln County War and am afraid to give up because my Enemies would Kill me. the day Mr. Chapman was murdered I was in Lincoln, at the request of good Citizens to meet Mr. J.J. Dolan to meet as Friends, so as to be able to lay aside our arms and go to Work. I was present when Mr. Chapman was murdered and know who did it and if it were not for those indictments I would have made it clear before now. if it is in your power to Annully those indictments I hope you will do so so as to give me a chance to explain. Please send me an awnser telling me what you can do You can send awnser by bearer I have no wish to fight any more indeed I have not raised an arm since your proclamation. As to my character I refer to any of the citizens, for the majority of them are my friends and have been helping me all they could. I am called Kid Antrim but Antrim is my stepfathers name.

Waiting for an awnser I remain your Obedeint Servant
W.H. Bonney

Governor Lew Wallace's reply to Billy the Kid's above letter:

Lincoln, March 15, 1879

W.H. Bonney,

Come to the house of old Squire Wilson (not the lawyer) at nine (9) o'clock next Monday night alone. I don't mean his office, but his residence. Follow along the foot of the mountain south of the town, come in on that side, and knock at the east door. I have authority to exempt you from prosecution, if you will testify to what you say you know.

The object of the meeting at Squire Wilson's is to arrange the matter in a way to make your life safe. To do that the utmost secrecy is to be used. <u>So come alone</u>. Don't tell anybody – not a living soul – where you are coming or the object. If you could trust Jesse Evans, you can trust me.

-Lew Wallace

Letter to Gov. Wallace from Billy in Santa Fe jail:

Santa Fe Jail New Mex
March 2d 1881

Gov. Lew Wallace
Dear Sir,

I wish you would come down to the jail and see me. it will be to your interest to come and see me. I have some letters which date back two years, and there are Parties who are very anxious to get them but I shall not dispose of them until I see you. that is if you will come imediately.

Yours Respect-
Wm H. Bonney

Letter March 13, 1879, W. H. Bonney to Governor Lew Wallace offering to name Chapman murderers.

If it is in your power to Annully
those indictments I hope you will do so
so a to give me a chance to explain.
please send me an answer telling me what
you can do You can send answer by bearer
I have no Wish to fight any more indeed
I have not raised an arm since your self Commenced
as to my Character I refer to any of
the Citizens. for the majority of them are
my Friends and have been helping me
all they could. I am Called Kid Antrim
but Antrim is my Stepfathers name.
    Writing an answer I remain
    Your Obedient Servant
                    W. H. Bonney

Letter March 15, 1879, Governor Lew Wallace replying to W. H. Bonney with prospect of exemption from prosecution.

Lincoln, March 15. 1879.

W. H. Bonney.

Come to the house of old Squire Wilson (not the lawyer) at nine (9) o'clock next Monday night alone. I don't mean his office, but his residence. Follow along the foot of the mountain south of the town, come in on that side, and knock at the east door. I have authority to exempt you from prosecution, if you will testify to what you say you know.

The object of the meeting at Squire Wilson's is to arrange the matter in a way to make your life safe. To do that the utmost secrecy is to be used. So come alone. Don't tell anybody — not a living soul — where you are coming or the object. If you could trust Jesse Evans, you can trust me.

Lew. Wallace.

Letter March 2, 1881, from W. H. Bonney in Santa Fe jail to Governor Lew Wallace.

Santa Fe jail New Mex
March 2d 1881

Gov. Lew Wallace
Dear Sir

I wish you would come down to the jail and see me. it will be to your interest to come and see me, I have some letters which date back two years, and there are Parties who are very anxious to get them, but I shall not dispose of them until I see you. that is if you will come imediatly

Yours Respect—
Wm H Bonney

Resources

Title page of Garrett book: *The Authentic Life of Billy, The Kid* by Pat. F. Garrett, New Mexican Printing and Publishing Co., Santa Fe, New Mexico, 1882.

Marriage entry for marriage of Catherine McCarty and William Antrim: Santa Fe (NM) County Marriage Records

Old Lincoln town: New Mexico State Records Center & Archives annotated by author

Order that William Bonney be hanged: New Mexico State Records Center & Archives

Lincoln courthouse showing Billy's cell window: author's photograph

Warrant not served, signed by Pat Garrett: New Mexico State Records Center and Archives, Santa Fe

Letter from Billy the Kid to Lew Wallace March 13, 1879: Fray Angelico Chavez Historical Library, Santa Fe, New Mexico, Lincoln County Heritage Trust, Lincoln, NM

Letter from Lew Wallace to Billy the Kid March 15, 1979: Lew Wallace papers, Indiana Historical Society

Letter from Billy the Kid to Lew Wallace, March 2, 1881: Fray Angelico Chavez Historical Library, Santa Fe, New Mexico, Lincoln County Heritage Trust, Lincoln, NM

CPSIA information can be obtained at www.ICGtesting.com
Printed in the USA
LVOW08s2250090614

389326LV00005B/126/P